Bubsy

Don Lemna

Cover and text illustrations
Sally J.K. Davies

Riverwood

Riverwood Publishers Ltd.
6 Donlands Avenue, P.O. Box 70
Sharon, Ontario L0G 1V0

P.O. Box 78306
St. Louis, MO 63178

Canadian Cataloguing In Publication Data

Lemna, Don, 1936–
    Bubsy

ISBN 1-895121-18-3

I. Davies, Sally J.K.   II. Title

PS8573.E548B83 1993 jC813'.54 C93-093977-8
PZ7.L45Bu 1993

Illustrations by Sally J.K. Davies
Design and typesetting by Heidy Lawrance Associates
Printed and bound in Canada by Webcom

I wish to dedicate this story to my grandchildren. In the order of their appearance on the planet, they are: Matthew, Joseph, Sean, Samantha and Robyn.

Chapter 1

Bubsy had fantastic news! He dropped his BMX under the birch tree and ran for the house as though he'd been shot from a gun.

As usual, his mother was in her basement art room, working on one of her paintings. This one looked like an exploding watermelon.

"Hey Mom, guess what! My story won the writing contest! It's the one about the funny raccoon, and Mrs. Neilsen said it was the best story! She gave me a Saint Bernard poster for winning." He held up the poster for her to look at. The huge dog stared placidly out at them.

"Oh Bubsy, that's wonderful!" his mother exclaimed.

After she'd hugged and kissed him, Bubsy left her to rejoice by herself and went off in search of the Second-In-Command. He looked all around the house, but there was no sign of his father.

Finally, out back, he spotted his dad's big feet lying in front of the garage. They were sticking out from under the car. Bubsy lay down on the ground and grinned over at him.

"Hey Dad, guess what?"

His father grunted in response.

"My story about the raccoon won the writing contest!" Bubsy exclaimed.

Mr. McGourlic's hand shot out from under the car. It shook Bubsy's hand and then disappeared again.

"You take after me," his father said proudly from down under.

Bubsy left him to celebrate by himself under there and headed upstairs to the room he shared with his older brother. He had his prize poster in his hand and he was positively glowing with pride. But when he opened the bedroom door, he saw something that instantly destroyed his happiness. He saw that his older brother had taken over the card table!

This card table belonged to Bubsy. It had always been his card table. It was where he did his homework and kept his books and school things. It was his personal place. But now the whole table was occupied by Steve's giant balsa wood model airplane.

And where were Bubsy's books and other things? Why Steve had dumped them all into a cardboard box! Even his precious and fragile "Snoopy" lamp had been taken off the table and thrown into the box.

It wasn't fair! Steve had the big desk by the window all to himself. He didn't need the card table too.

Bubsy stared at the offending airplane. He wanted to throw it out the window. The only thing that stopped him was this strange desire he had to go on living. Steve had been working on that model for months, and Bubsy knew that if he threw it out the window, his brother would throw him out the window. Steve could do it too. He was big. Very big. What's more, Steve was in Junior High, so he had a bad temper. Bubsy was only in grade five, so he wasn't allowed to have a bad temper.

He turned away from Steve's airplane and unrolled his Saint Bernard poster. He then searched the bedroom walls for a place to hang it up. But there wasn't any place. No place at all, because the walls were covered top to bottom with Steve's huge posters of his favorite rock groups.

It isn't fair! Bubsy though angrily. It's my room too!

He then made a daring decision. He would make room for his poster.

Mustering his courage, he climbed on a chair and carefully took down one of Steve's posters. He hid it in the back of the closet and then he put his Saint Bernard poster in its place. When he was finished, he stepped back to admire the bold thing he'd done. There, right in the centre of the wall, completely surrounded by rock bands, the big dog sat quietly staring out at the world.

He wondered what Steve would do when he saw it. Would he get mad and tear the poster to shreds? If he did, Bubsy decided, he would definitely throw Steve's airplane out the window. Even though it would mean instant death, he would do it.

Bubsy now began to feel a little depressed. He was rather tired as well, so he climbed the ladder up to his bed. But when he got to the top, he discovered there were piles of Steve's airplane model magazines all over his bunk. He was just about to remove them when the door opened and Steve came in.

"Don't touch my magazines!" Steve warned.

"But I want to lie down," Bubsy protested.

"You'll have to wait until I'm finished sorting them out," his brother replied.

"Then I'll use your bunk," Bubsy said as he climbed down the ladder.

"Dick's coming over to listen to my new tape," Steve informed him. "So you have to get lost."

"I won't! It's my room too!" Bubsy declared loudly. He thereupon threw himself onto the lower bunk and curled up into a ball in the corner.

At that moment the door opened and Dick came in. Dick was Steve's best friend. He was in Junior High with Steve, so he also had a bad temper.

"Hey, what's up?" Dick asked.

"The little nerd won't leave, so it looks like we'll have to heave him out," Steve said with a grin at his friend. He then seized one of Bubsy's legs and tried to drag him off the bunk. Bubsy kicked fiercely at Steve's hands with his other leg, but the ever helpful Dick grabbed the kicking leg and held it.

The two boys pulling together were far too strong for Bubsy. They could have ripped him right off the bunk, if they'd wanted to. But they were content to pull him off slowly, so they could enjoy his furious squeals of protest. It is an established fact that Junior High boys have a weird sense of humour—in addition to their bad tempers.

Slowly but surely they dragged Bubsy toward the edge of the bunk. But he wasn't going to give up easily. He reached out and clutched the end of the mattress. Not that it did him any good. The mattress wasn't attached to anything, so it simply came with him.

At the last moment, just when Bubsy and the mattress were about to hit the floor together, he grabbed one of the bunk bed's corner posts and held on with all his might. Steve and Dick only laughed at him. They continued to pull on his legs until he was stretched out from the post like a living clothesline. But Bubsy held on as hard as he could, and now the bunk bed was starting to move.

"Grab his arms," Dick suggested. "I'll hang onto the legs."

After Steve gave the left leg to Dick, he pulled Bubsy's hands off the post and seized him under the armpits. The two older boys then carried the squealing ball of fury into the hallway.

"Let me go! Let me go!"

Even though Bubsy was as mad as he could possibly get, almost to the point of frothing at the mouth, they completely ignored him. Nor did it bother them in the least that he was twisting and squirming like a wounded alligator. They were both laughing like demented hyenas, as if the whole thing were a big joke.

They carried him down to the far end of the hallway and dropped him in front of his older sister Beth's bedroom door. Then they headed back down to the hall, cackling loudly as they went.

The door behind Bubsy opened and Beth stared down at him. "What on earth is going on!?" she asked angrily.

"They threw me out of the bedroom," Bubsy informed her.

"Oh, when are you idiots going to grow up!" she exclaimed as she retreated back into her room, slamming the door behind her.

Bubsy picked himself up and walked back to the bedroom. Loud music and cackling laughter were flooding out from under the door and he felt himself getting angry all over again. After all, it was his room too.

He decided he was going back into that room and he was going to stay there, whether they liked it or not. He opened the door and boldly walked in.

"He's back," Dick observed.

"Not for long," Steve grinned.

"It's my room too!" Bubsy shouted defiantly.

Steve and Dick merely looked at each other and smiled. Then the two older boys seized Bubsy by various parts of his body and dumped him back in the hallway. He jumped quickly to his feet and tried to open the door again, but they pushed it shut against him. Then they put a chair under the doorknob so he couldn't open it at all.

A lesser person might have felt a little discouraged at this point, but Bubsy wasn't the kind of kid to give up without a good fight. He lay down next to the door and put his feet up against the doorjamb. They would have to come out sometime. They would have to come out to go to the bathroom. They would have to come out to get something to eat. And as soon as they opened the door, he would crawl into the room before they could stop him. Yes, he'd scurry right between their legs and hide under the bottom bunk among all the boxes. They would never get him out from under there.

While he was waiting for the door to open, he started to think about Cathy Chung. A month ago she'd moved here from somewhere out East and now she lived in a house almost directly across the alley from him. She was an expert on the skateboard. He'd watched her work out on the ramps down in Kin Coulee and he'd been quite impressed with her skill. He hoped that one of these days he'd get up enough nerve to talk to her.

For a long time he just lay there, listening to the howling music coming from the other side of the door. Whenever it died down, he could hear Steve and Dick talking about girls. It was all very boring, and presently Bubsy fell asleep. He slept soundly, even though he was still lying in the doorway with his feet up against the doorjamb. When you're eleven years old you're still fairly flexible and can sleep almost anywhere.

Sometime later, Dick opened the door and came out. He was on his way to the bathroom. However, he didn't get very far because he tripped over Bubsy, who was still lying in the doorway. Dick then went careering headfirst across the hallway, and such was his speed that it looked like he might never stop. But he did come to a stop. He came to a stop very suddenly, when his head met the opposite wall and disappeared into it.

"Look what you've done!" Steve screamed. "You've killed him!"

Chapter 2

"What's happening?" Beth yelled. She came running out of her bedroom, but when she saw Dick sticking out of the wall she stopped suddenly and blinked hard.

"Why is he doing that?" she asked.

"Bubsy killed him!" Steve cried out hysterically. "He was my best friend!"

While Bubsy stared fearfully at Dick's rear end, Steve leaped down the stairs to find their father.

"Is he really dead?" Beth asked in a puzzled voice.

"Get me out!" Dick screamed.

"He isn't dead," Bubsy informed her.

"Oh Lord!" Beth exclaimed. "You guys are hopeless!"

The scream had come from the other side of the wall, so Bubsy opened the door to the master bedroom and looked inside. Dick's head was sticking through into the room.

"His head is in here," Bubsy announced.

He stared at the head. It looked like it had been mounted on the wall, only it was a lot lower than heads are usually mounted.

"I can't get out!" Dick said quietly. "My head won't go back through."

At that moment Bubsy's father came running up the stairs. He stopped dead in his tracks when he saw Dick sticking in the wall.

"See! He's killed my best friend!" Steve shrieked.

"He isn't dead," Bubsy said. "His head is just in the next room."

After looking at Dick's rear end with stunned disbelief, Mr. McGourlic got down on his hands and knees and broke away some of the plasterboard below Dick's neck. A moment later Dick was free and he didn't seem to be hurt at all. In fact, his head was grinning stupidly when it came out of the wall.

At that moment, Bubsy's mother appeared on the landing below them.

"Where's supper?" she asked.

"It isn't ready yet," Mr. McGourlic replied in a weary voice. It was his turn to make supper. "We

have a little problem here," he explained.

When Mrs. McGourlic came up the rest of the way and saw the hole in the wall, she gasped with astonishment.

"It's going to take me a whole day to fix it," Mr. McGourlic moaned.

"I think I'm getting a headache," Dick decided.

"Then go home and take some aspirin," Beth suggested.

"How on earth did it happen?" Mrs. McGourlic asked.

"He did it," Steve informed them, moving an accusing finger up and down over Bubsy's head. "He tripped Dick when he was coming out of my bedroom."

"Oh Bubsy, why would you do a thing like that?" his mother asked, shaking her head sadly at him.

"I didn't mean to!" Bubsy protested. "It wasn't my fault!"

He tried to explain it to them, but Steve kept interrupting him and twisting things around.

"They're both idiots," Beth said helpfully.

In the end, although Bubsy was at least able to make them understand that he hadn't deliberately tripped Dick, they still blamed him for the hole in the wall. "It was an accident waiting to happen," his father said, frowning down at him. "After this, don't sleep in doorways."

This had been the day of Bubsy's greatest triumph—the day he'd won the first writing prize he'd ever won in all his life. But now his parents were mad at him and it was all spoiled.

Later, as he lay on his bunk, Bubsy thought about the person who'd once again ruined things for him. He was almost used to it—used to having his older brother destroy whatever bit of happiness might happen to come his way.

He opened his eyes and looked over at Steve. He was sitting at the card table, busily working on his beloved model and humming happily to himself. The hole in the wall was already forgotten.

Bubsy turned on his back and closed his eyes. But even though he was worn out, for some reason he couldn't fall asleep. He opened his eyes again and just lay there staring at the ceiling.

In order to raise his spirits, he tried to think of something pleasant. At first he couldn't come up with anything, but then he remembered his precious collection of Peanuts books. He owned seven of them, all neatly stored in the closet in a cardboard box. He would have liked to keep his Peanuts books out where he could see them, but there was no room for them in the bedroom bookcase. All its eight shelves were filled with Steve's books and magazines.

When he got tired of staring at the ceiling, Bubsy turned on his side and gazed absently across the room. Then he noticed something that made him sit bolt upright. His Saint Bernard poster was gone from the wall.

"Where's my poster!" he shouted.

"Don't get your hair in a knot. I didn't hurt your stupid poster," Steve replied without looking up from his model.

"Then where is it?" Bubsy cried.

"It's in the closet."

Bubsy rushed to the closet and found it. With his heart thumping wildly, he unrolled the poster and checked it over. It had not been damaged.

"Why can't I put it up?" he asked.

"Because it gives me the creeps," Steve said with a shudder. "I don't like dogs."

Steve was not lying. He really didn't like dogs. When he was a small boy, he'd run into one so completely covered with long hair that he could not tell which end of it was which. And while he was talking to one end of the dog, the other end turned around and bit him. Actually the dog had only nipped the end of his nose, but ever since then Steve had been afraid of dogs. Certainly the last thing he would want was a poster of an enormous Saint Bernard staring down at him from the middle of the bedroom wall.

"But it's only a picture," Bubsy protested.

"I don't care. I don't like dogs and I don't like pictures of dogs either," Steve said bitterly.

"If I get a poster that isn't a dog, can I put it up?" Bubsy asked.

"No, you can't," Steve said firmly. "Now go away and stop bothering me!"

"But you've got all your posters on the walls," Bubsy persisted. "I only want to put up one. Why can't I?"

"Because mine were there first," Steve replied gruffly. "Now leave me alone! I'm busy!"

"You always get everything," Bubsy moaned. Actually, it was a cross between a whine and a moan.

"I'm older than you," Steve muttered. Then

he gave Bubsy a threatening glance. "And don't go whining to Mom and Dad, if you know what's good for you."

"Yeah? What'll you do about it?" Bubsy challenged.

"I'll break every corpuscle in your puny body, for starters," Steve replied, holding his bony fist up for his brother's inspection.

"You wouldn't dare hurt me," Bubsy scoffed.

"No? Try it and see. And after I've broken you into little pieces, I'll tell everybody you're a nerd ratfink. Including Cathy Chung," he added with a sly smile.

"You rotten… You wouldn't!"

Steve chuckled to himself, then smirked at Bubsy.

"What would dear Cathy-Wathy think if she heard little Bubsy-Wubsy was a nerd ratfink who goes whining to his mommy and daddy every time he can't get his way? What would she think, eh?"

A hundred times during the last week Bubsy had regretted that in a moment of weakness he'd told his brother he liked Cathy Chung. It was such a stupid thing to do! But he'd done it and now Steve teased him about her at every opportunity. He glared at his brother with hot fury and promised himself he'd never again share any of his secrets with him. Not ever. Never!

"Suppertime!" Mr. McGourlic called from downstairs.

"Is it okay for me to eat supper?" Bubsy asked sarcastically.

"Be my guest," Steve replied with a sneer.

"We're having hamburgers tonight," Beth said on the way down.

Bubsy sat patiently at his place as his father served the hamburgers and fries. After his mother said grace, he ate his hamburger and it tasted great. Now it was time to start on the fries. But first he needed some ketchup.

"Pass the ketchup, please," he said politely.

No one heard him. They were all busy arguing about his aunt Kate, which is something they often did at mealtimes…

"The trouble with Kate is that she carries everything to extremes. She's becoming a real nut case," his father loudly declared.

"How can you say things like that? Kate is your own sister!" Mrs. McGourlic exclaimed. "And what's more, I think she's marvelous with all she does. People love her. At least some people do."

"I do," Bubsy said.

"I don't," Steve muttered while casually picking with his fingernail at a sliver of food that was stuck between his front teeth.

"Kate McGourlic may be my sister, but she's still a royal pain in the butt," Mr. McGourlic growled.

"Now, if that isn't an awful thing to say!" Mrs. McGourlic hotly responded. "Kate is a loving, compassionate woman who's devoted her life to helping disadvantaged people."

"She's still a poop-disturber," Mr. McGourlic muttered.

"Well, you can say what you want about her," Mrs. McGourlic responded angrily, "but it won't alter the truth. She's a saint!"

"And Kate's a wonderful actress too," Beth broke in.

"I never said she wasn't a good actress," Mr. McGourlic snapped.

"That's not the point. Kate is…well, she's got no restraint. With her, it's just one thing after another. Heaven knows what her next cause will be!"

"Pass the ketchup, please," Bubsy asked again. The bottle was sitting on the other side of the table, right beside Steve's plate. Steve looked at the ketchup bottle and then grinned at Bubsy. He obviously wasn't going to pass it to him, so Bubsy gave up and reached for it himself. Unfortunately, while he was stretching across the table, his elbow hit his glass of milk. The glass tipped over and the milk flooded across Beth's plate. It splashed into her lap in a white tidal wave.

"YEEK!!!" she screamed. She ran to the sink and began to wipe furiously at her dress with a teatowel while Steve looked on with an expression of supreme delight on his face.

"Bubsy! Look what you've done!" his mother exclaimed as she rushed for the dishcloth.

"I was just trying to get the ketchup," Bubsy explained.

"Next time try asking for it, instead of reaching across the table," Mr. McGourlic suggested with a frown.

"I did!" Bubsy protested. "I asked Steve, but he—"

"I didn't hear him," Steve interrupted.

"The little idiot's ruined this dress!" Beth

exclaimed as she went upstairs to change into something dry.

"See all the trouble he causes," Steve muttered with a half-concealed smile.

"Don't you know it's bad manners to reach across the table?" his mother asked Bubsy as she wiped up the milk from around Beth's plate.

He looked across the table at Steve and once again, for maybe the millionth time, Bubsy wondered what it would be like to have a brother who liked him and helped him, instead of one who hated him and was always trying to make his life miserable. But what was the use of dreaming?

After supper Bubsy felt very sad, so he decided to go over and visit his Aunt Kate. He hadn't seen her for awhile and she always managed to give his spirits a lift. He grabbed his raccoon story and wandered outside into the cool evening air.

Chapter 3

Bubsy's aunt Kate lived in a nearby apartment block, just at the top of the hill. A few minutes after he'd set out from home, Bubsy was sitting on her sofa eating cookies while she read his story. Kate always gave him something good to eat when he visited her. It was one of the reasons she was so likeable.

Twice she laughed out loud while she read the story. When she was finished, she smiled at him and her smile was warm and encouraging.

"It's a perfectly lovely story," she said. "I can see why it won the contest."

"I got a Saint Bernard poster for winning," he proudly informed her. Then he frowned.

"What's the matter?"

"Steve won't let me put it on the wall. He doesn't like dogs. But even if I had a poster that wasn't a dog, he wouldn't let me put it up."

"Why not?"

"He says there isn't room. The walls are all covered with his rock posters," Bubsy explained.

"The selfish boy!" she said.

She looked at Bubsy more closely. "You seem very unhappy, darling," she said to him. She sat on the arm of the sofa and caressed his head with her soft hand.

Bubsy poured out his heart. He told her everything that had happened from the moment he'd come home from school until he'd left the house to visit her. She did giggle a little when he told her about Dick getting stuck in the wall; but by the time he'd come to the part about spilling his milk because Steve wouldn't pass him the ketchup, Kate looked very sad. She reached over and hugged him tightly.

"My poor darling," she sighed, gently stroking his hair. "You're being oppressed. Steve is completely ignoring your needs and rights as a person."

Before he could ask her what she meant by this, Kate excused herself and went into the kitchen to make a phone call.

While his aunt was on the phone, Bubsy wandered around the huge room and looked at her theatre posters. Kate was an actress and a director at The Free Women's Theatre. It was down on North Railway Avenue, next to Gino's Shoe Repair.

After he got tired of looking at posters, he moved along her wall of bookshelves, inspecting the hundreds and hundreds of books that lined it. Right in front of him were two long shelves that contained nothing but books of poetry.

He was always slightly amazed that anyone could own so many books. But he knew how much Kate loved to read. She had once told him that many of the happiest moments in her life came when she was curled up in her armchair reading a good book.

He wandered over to her working corner and began to absent-mindedly push the keys down on her computer. Kate was writing a play on this computer. In fact, she'd written many plays on it over the years. Bubsy had even seen her acting in some of them, though he hadn't really enjoyed the experience. Not that she wasn't a good actress. She was a very good actress. The trouble was that her female characters suffered a lot, and

Bubsy found it hard to watch them weep.

After Kate was through with her phone call, she came over to Bubsy and gave him a pat on the head.

"Come on, get your jacket," she smiled.

"Why? Where are we going?" he asked her with a puzzled look.

"We're going to a movie," Kate informed him.

"We are? But…"

"It's my special treat to you for winning the story contest. And I've cleared it with your mom and dad, so just relax and enjoy yourself."

The movie they went to was a very funny comedy. For an hour and a half, Bubsy laughed and laughed. So did his aunt. He also ate a tub of buttered popcorn, two Crispy Crunch chocolate bars, and he drank two medium cokes. So did his aunt.

As they drove home after the movie, just as they were turning the corner onto Belfast Street, the moonlight swept across Kate's face and lit it up. Her nose was rather big and she was not at all pretty, but that didn't matter to Bubsy—nor to any of the people who knew her. She could dance and sing and write plays and act and she was a brilliant woman. Everybody said so. She was also very kind. And generous. And loving.

"When you feel like talking some more, just come on over," Kate said as she stopped the truck in front of his house.

"Thanks for taking me to the movie," he said. "I really liked it."

"I always enjoy your company," she replied. "Besides, I felt like celebrating tonight. I've had a bit of luck. They're going to produce one of my plays in the Northwest Drama Festival.

"Will you be rich?" Bubsy asked. The idea of having a rich aunt who loved him had a certain appeal.

"Oh no," Kate laughed. "Not rich. But I'll be able to pay my rent for awhile."

When Bubsy closed his eyes that night, he could hear Steve snorting down below like a stuffed-up pig. But he was so used to Steve's awful sleeping noises that he hardly heard them anymore. Besides, he had other things on his mind. He was thinking about the wonderful evening he'd just had.

Maybe life wasn't so bad, after all.

Chapter 4

On Monday after school, Bubsy and his friend Milton sat on the bedroom floor with a large pile of magazines stacked up between them. They were looking for pictures of different kinds of pollution to put in a collage. It was a homework assignment for Mr. Gale's Social Studies class.

"Here's one," Milton said. He held it up for Bubsy to see.

It was a picture of something that had once been a seabird, but now it was hard to tell what it was. From the bottom of its small webbed feet to the tip of its beak, the little creature was covered with thick, tarry oil. A tiny eye gazed dimly out at them from the lump of blackness it had become. Its suffering was almost over.

"It makes you want to cry," Bubsy sighed.

Milton nodded sadly at his friend. He picked

up the scissors and began to cut out the picture.

"What kind of bird is it?" Bubsy asked, taking up his notebook.

For each picture they used in the collage, they had to supply the answers to five important questions: Who? What? Where? When? and Why?

Some of the answers were easily found. The caption under the picture said the bird was a Cormorant. The first paragraph of the article informed them that it was standing on a beach in Kuwait. The article went on to say that the polluting, killing oil had been deliberately released into the Persian Gulf by soldiers from Iraq. They were carrying out the orders of their leader, Saddam Hussein. It made Bubsy sick to think that anyone would do such a terrible thing on purpose.

Just as Milton finished cutting out the picture of the dying bird, the door opened and Steve walked in. When he saw what they were doing, a scowl appeared on his face.

"Clear out!" he ordered.

"We're working on a project for school," Bubsy protested.

"I don't care what you're doing, Nerd. Get out!

I'm going to work on my model and I don't want you wimps bothering me."

"We'll be quiet," Milton promised. "We're just looking for pictures."

"Out!" Steve screamed. He gave their stack of magazines a kick and scattered them across the floor.

"I'm going to get Mom!" Bubsy yelled, leaping to his feet.

"No you're not. Mom and Dad went to the library," Steve said with a nasty grin. "So pick up your junk and get lost. Or else…"

"Or else what!?" Bubsy challenged.

"Or else I'll turf you out!" Steve threatened.

"Just try it!" Bubsy shouted defiantly.

A second later Steve had him in a headlock and was dragging him toward the door.

"I'll get him!" Milton cried, whereupon he leaped onto Steve's back like an enraged monkey. Taking advantage of Steve's surprise, Bubsy broke free from the headlock and grabbed his brother around the legs. The fight was on!

Although Steve struggled furiously to get them off him, Bubsy and Milton clung to him like a pair of determined little leeches. Now off balance, Steve staggered sideways until he hit the card table.

"Wait. WAIT!!" he cried. He stopped struggling and stood perfectly still. "Just wait a minute, you guys," he said, speaking very calmly. "We can't fight in here. We'll break my model."

"Who cares?" Milton asked. He was still fastened tightly to Steve's back.

"I'll tell you what," Steve said soothingly. "Let me go and we'll fight it out down on the lawn."

"Why should we?" Bubsy demanded. "We've got you beat." He was still locked securely to Steve's legs.

"Okay, I'll make a deal with you," Steve said in his friendliest tone of voice. "If you agree to fight down on the lawn, you guys can start with the same holds you've got on me now. And whoever wins gets to use the bedroom."

"How do we know you'll keep your word?" Bubsy asked.

"May God destroy my model, if I lie," Steve said with one hand solemnly on his heart.

At that moment Bubsy had a bright idea...

"Let him go," he said to Milton. As he spoke, he released his brother's legs and then Milton dropped from his back. Steve then turned his fierce eyes on the two of them.

"Okay you wimps," he hissed. "Down to the backyard! I'm going to crunch you both!"

"You go ahead," Bubsy suggested. "We'll meet you there in two minutes. We just want to pick up our magazines."

"All right," Steve growled. "Pick them up and then get down there! I'll be waiting for you!" He hit his fist into his palm and smiled fiendishly as he went out.

"He won't let us get those holds on him," Milton predicted, after Steve had gone. "We had him beat and you let him go."

"It doesn't matter," Bubsy replied. He then shoved the straight chair under the doorknob. "Now he can't bother us anymore," he said with a grin.

They went to the bedroom window and looked down at the backyard. Steve was standing under the fir tree in the middle of the lawn, patiently waiting for them to come down. His eyes were fastened on the back door.

"He's not so smart," Bubsy said with a grin.

"We could take him," Milton responded. "It

would be two against one."

But Bubsy knew better. Even if Steve let them get the same holds on him that they'd had before, there was no chance they would win. Out there in the open, where his precious model was not endangered, Steve would be able to fight freely. Out there he would tear them apart.

They watched him go over and sit down on the concrete lip of the goldfish pond. It had not yet occurred to him that he'd been outsmarted by his little brother. His eyes did not move from the back door. He was still waiting for them to appear.

"Now we can work in peace," Bubsy smiled, turning away from the window.

"I still say we could beat him," Milton commented.

"Not a chance," Bubsy said, shaking his head. "We'd both wind up in the fish pond."

"We could take him," Milton insisted. "I'd just grab him like this—"As he spoke, Milton sprang on Bubsy from behind. He tightened his arm a little around his friend's neck to show what he meant.

Bubsy's reaction was totally instinctive. He

reached back over his shoulder and grabbed the upper part of Milton's arm—the one Milton had around his neck. Then, using his back to take Milton's weight, he suddenly bent down and flipped his friend over his shoulder. Milton landed on his butt and his feet slammed the bookcase. There was a startled expression on his face. He was not hurt, but he was very surprised.

However, Bubsy was not looking at his friend right then. His eyes were on the bookcase. It had been tipped slightly by the impact of Milton's feet and now something big was wobbling about on the top left-hand corner—something big and round and brightly coloured. Bubsy's eyes focused and he recognized it. It was Steve's big metal globe of the world, which Grampa McGourlic had given him last Christmas. It was teetering at the very edge.

Then it fell.

Bubsy watched with great interest as the globe toppled off the shelf. But his fascination turned to horror when it landed right on the tail of Steve's giant airplane model.

"It broke your brother's plane!" Milton exclaimed as he got to his feet.

34

Bubsy didn't reply. He just stood there, staring in wide-eyed horror at the bits of balsa wood that had once been the tail of Steve's beloved model.

"What's the matter?" Milton asked. He waved his hand in front of Bubsy's staring eyes, but there was no immediate response.

"Bubsy? What's the matter with you?" he asked again.

This time there was a flicker of life in Bubsy's eyes and his lips moved ever so slightly. They definitely seemed to be trying to say something, but Milton couldn't make out what it was. Then the words finally came out...

"I'm dead," Bubsy whispered hoarsely.

"What?"

"He's going to kill me," Bubsy said in an agonized voice.

He ran to the window and looked anxiously down. Steve was still sitting on the edge of the goldfish pond, waiting impatiently for them to come down and fight.

"Just the tail's broken," Milton said from over by the card table.

"It doesn't matter. I'm dead," Bubsy moaned.

"Maybe you can fix it before he finds out," Milton suggested.

A flicker of hope shot through Bubsy's mind. Maybe there was a chance! Maybe, just maybe… He rushed to the card table and began to hurriedly examine the damaged tail.

It didn't look good. The tail was smashed almost beyond recognition. But at least the bits and pieces were still there. Maybe it would be possible to glue them back together.

"Go watch him," he said to Milton.

As Milton went to the window to keep watch, Bubsy bent over the table and collected all the bits of balsa wood into a pile. There was a tail in there somewhere, but how did all these fragments of it fit together? He examined the model's blueprint for a minute, then picked up the airplane glue. Well, why not give it a try? What did he have to lose?

A minute later he was hard at work, gluing the pieces of the tail back together as best he could. If only he didn't have to rush at it. If only he knew what he was doing! Already he could see that his repairs would not be perfect. Well, maybe his brother wouldn't notice. However, all the while he worked so feverishly, in his quivering heart he knew the truth. Steve would notice. There was no doubt about it, for the reconstruction was now beginning to resemble a piece of modern art rather than the tail of an airplane.

"He's coming back!" Milton warned from the window.

Bubsy moaned with dismay and tried to work faster. But it was very difficult. His hands were shaking and he'd lost his concentration. Nothing seemed to be working out. It was a mess. He was a mess too. His fingers were coated with glue and there were tiny bits of balsa wood stuck all over them.

The doorknob turned and there was a muffled grunt from outside the room. Someone was trying to open the door.

"Hey, what's going on!?" Steve shouted at them through the door. "I thought you chickens wanted to fight!"

"Go away," Bubsy said nervously. "We're working on our project."

"Let me in, you wimps!" Steve yelled. He began to thump and pound on the door, which made it difficult for Bubsy to concentrate on what he was doing. He glanced over and saw that the chair had slipped a little under his brother's hammering.

"Hold the chair!" he screamed at Milton.

Milton ran to the chair and held it fast.

"What are you guys doing in there?" Steve shouted. "Let me in or I'm really going to get mad!"

"What's he like when he gets mad?" Milton asked.

"You don't want to be here," Bubsy answered fearfully as he tried to fit another piece of balsa wood into place on the tail—or whatever it was.

Now Steve began to throw his whole weight against the door. Even with Milton doing his best to hold it in place, the chair was forced back a little.

"I can't hold it much longer," he warned.

At that precise moment, the whole airplane tail happened to be stuck to Bubsy's left hand. When he tried to remove it with his other hand, it stuck to his other hand.

Now the pounding at the door turned into a horrendous thunder that threatened to bring the whole house down—that is, if the door didn't break first. Under these circumstances, and with the airplane tail sticking first to one hand and then to the other, it was very difficult for Bubsy to make any progress at all.

"I can't do it!!" he screamed, leaping up from the table.

Chapter 5

While Steve continued to thud like a pile driver against the door, Bubsy and Milton rushed to the far side of the room and threw open the window. Bubsy climbed out of it first. Holding onto the sill, he lowered himself as far as possible, then dropped onto the back porch roof. Milton followed quickly and the two of them scampered down the side of the porch. A second later they stood together on the lawn, looking up at the window. Suddenly the noise of Steve crashing against the door ceased.

"He got in," Milton announced.

"Maybe he won't see it," Bubsy said hopefully. He closed his eyes and listened.

There followed a moment of eerie silence, then a piercing, high-pitched scream shattered the air.

"AHHHHHHHHHHHH!!"

"He saw it," Bubsy said.

A second later, Steve appeared at the window. He stared down at them. His face was pale as death, but his eyes were burning like molten lava...

"Now you die," he said in a low hissing voice.

With amazing speed and agility, he thrust himself through the window and dropped onto the porch roof.

"Run for your life!" Bubsy shrieked.

They raced frantically around the side of the house, almost tripping over each other in their haste to escape. By now Steve was on the ground and racing after them.

At the side gate, Bubsy and Milton bumped against each other and three precious seconds were wasted while they fumbled furiously to open the latch. By the time they were through the gate, Steve was only a few steps away. He would surely have caught them, except that Bubsy had the presence of mind to slam the gate behind him.

Steve ran into the gate. In fact, he hit it so hard that he bounced backwards and wound up on his rear end. By the time he'd recovered, Bubsy and Milton had their crash helmets on and were running down the street alongside their bicycles. Two seconds later, they were pedaling for their lives. From behind them came a roar of dismay…

"You won't get away!" Steve screamed.

But they did get away. They flew down street after street, until they'd left the raging fiend far behind. The two friends smiled at each other as they cut across the high school football field. They'd made it! They'd escaped!

When they reached the far side of the field, they dropped their bikes and flopped down on the grass to catch their breath.

"That was close!" Bubsy wheezed, using his sleeve to wipe the sweat off his forehead.

"He would've killed us," Milton gasped as he looked back across the football field.

"I've never seen him so mad before," Bubsy said with a worried glance at this friend.

"He's crazy," Milton panted.

"He loves that airplane more than anything," Bubsy said. He wiped his forehead again and felt something on his hand. There was still a small piece of balsa wood glued to it.

Bubsy stared blankly at the fragment of balsa wood and then, without quite knowing why, he started to laugh. The broken airplane. His frenzied attempt to fix it. The crazed monster at the window. The furious chase and the narrow escape … It all just seemed funny somehow. Soon both he and Milton were rolling around on the grass, laughing their heads off. A few minutes later, when their mirth had finally sputtered out, they lay quietly on their backs, breathing the fresh air and staring at the cloudless sky. The grass felt cool and soft beneath them.

"He's still going to kill you," Milton commented absently.

"I know," Bubsy responded. "But he has to catch me first."

"He will," Milton predicted.

At this they burst into a fresh fit of laughter.

While they lay on their backs, gazing at the sky and laughing at nothing, a lean, hard-looking teenager on a gleaming, black, California racing bicycle silently appeared on the sidewalk at the far corner of the football field. He paused for a moment. There was a tense expression on his pale face as his narrowed eyes slowly scanned the area. Like those of a hungry beast, the eyes were searching for something—or someone. A second later, the slitted eyes stopped moving and a gleam of dark triumph appeared in them. A hard, sinister smile spread itself across the boy's dry lips as he quietly turned his bike onto the field and began to ride silently across it, gathering speed as he went. He was headed for two specks lying on the grass on the other side.

They didn't know he was coming. They didn't see him. But when Steve was nearly halfway across the field, Bubsy sensed the presence of danger. Something was wrong! He sat bolt upright and gazed with horror at the terrifying spectre racing toward them.

"It's him!"

A second later the two of them were pedaling like maniacs down Seventh Street. Steve was now only a short distance behind them and gaining ground with every second that passed. On their thick, squat, BMX bikes they were no match for the avenging demon on his thin-tired California racing machine. Bubsy had a feeling it would be over in a few seconds. But he didn't give up.

"Go left at the corner," he gasped at Milton.

"Wait till I shout 'go!', then hit your breaks hard and peel off."

When they were nearly across the intersection, just at the instant when Steve was reaching out to grab him, Bubsy shouted "GO!". He and milton then applied their brakes for all they were worth and executed perfect skidding turns that sent them in opposite directions down Fifth Avenue.

Poor Steve. His black racer was much less maneuverable than the BMXs and his speed was very great. And, of course, he was totally unprepared for their sudden change in direction. He was through the intersection and nearly halfway down the next block before he'd fully realized what had happened.

"I'll get you!" he screamed in frustration, when finally he'd managed to slow down enough to do a U-turn.

By this time Bubsy was nearly two blocks south, racing away from him like a frightened rabbit from a mad wolf. He made a quick right turn and streaked up Ninth Street, just narrowly avoiding a head-on collision with a city garbage truck. It was then he discovered that his brakes were no longer working very well.

At the next corner he looked back. There was no sign of his brother. A tremendous feeling of relief swept over him. He'd won! He'd escaped!

His joy and relief were short-lived. For when he looked back again, he saw the black racing bike whip around the corner just a block behind him.

Steve was bent very low on his machine in order to reduce his air resistance and gain extra speed. In fact, his upper body was almost down to the crossbar and his legs were whirling around on the pedals like a pair of eggbeaters gone berserk.

Bubsy let out a little shriek of dismay and commanded his legs to pump for their lives. He turned left at the next corner, then did a sudden left turn into a back alley, hoping that the gravel and ruts in there might slow his brother down. They did slow Steve down a little, but not much. Without hesitating for a second, Bubsy raced across the street and into the next alley. But Steve continued to gain ground on him. Bubsy glanced back, then frantically wheeled to the right at the end of the alley, and tore down

47

Fifth Avenue. But Steve turned soon after him. It seemed hopeless. It was hopeless.

Or was it? Bubsy suddenly realized where he was and his mind clicked into high gear. There might still be a chance. He swung left at the next corner and streaked down a dead end street. Straight ahead of him was the edge of a hill and the beginning of a steep road which led down into the Kingsway area.

Suicide Road, it was called.

It was the kids who had named it Suicide Road. It really wasn't a road at all, just a rough trail that went almost straight down the long, steep hill. In fact, it was so rough and so very steep that no one in his right mind would ever attempt to ride down it on a bike. Especially not on a bike with brakes that weren't working too well. However, Bubsy knew it was the only way he could escape from the avenging devil on the black machine. He knew that Steve would never risk ruining his beloved racing bike by going down Suicide Road. But Bubsy, with his rugged BMX under him, thought he could make it.

As far as he knew, no one had ever attempted to ride down Suicide Road before. This would be a first. As he raced forward, he thought about what a story he'd have to tell later. It would make him famous.

"You're going to die," said a horrid panting voice.

The voice was just behind him, coming up fast. Bubsy leaped the concrete curb at the end of the street without even slowing down and raced furiously across the rough prairie grass. He was now aimed directly at the edge of the hill where the killer road began. He propelled himself toward it with all his energy and all his force. He was not thinking anymore. His only desire was to make it to the edge of the hill before Steve caught him.

Out of the corner of his eye he saw his brother again coming up alongside of him. As if he were caught in a horrifying nightmare, he saw his brother's long arm reach out for him. He ducked away from it and veered to the right just in time. And then suddenly he was over the edge, racing down Suicide Road. He heard Steve scream at him with rage and frustration from the top of the hill, but it didn't matter. Only one thing mattered...

He'd escaped! He was free!

However there was a slight problem. Suicide Road was even steeper than he remembered. Much steeper.

Down, down, down, he went, faster and faster and faster. He heard the wind whistling in his ears and by now he had made an interesting discovery. His brakes were definitely not working well.

"Help!!" Bubsy cried.

Faster and faster he went, down, down, down...

He was about to break the sound barrier. He thought he was. And now he was approaching the one curve in the trail—the place where it jogged suddenly to the left before continuing its downward path. The big question was—would he make the curve? The big answer was—no, he wouldn't.

He didn't have a hope. At the speed he was traveling, he couldn't even begin to make the turn.

Bubsy's eyes opened wide with fright as he went straight off the lip of the road, exactly like a jet going off the flight deck of an aircraft carrier. For a moment right then, he was actually flying through the air on his bike.

Nobody's ever done this before, he thought stupidly as he looked at the ground far below.

There was only time for this one thought, then Bubsy and his bicycle dropped out of the sky.

Chapter 6

When he opened his eyes, he discovered he was still alive. But just barely. He was dangling upside down from a branch in a huge willow tree, high above the ground. Down below were the remains of his BMX. Up above were a number of broken branches.

He felt like he'd been hit in the stomach by a sledgehammer. It took his breath away. When he tried to move, a terrible pain shot up his leg. There was also an awful stabbing sensation shooting down his arm. Then he noticed that his nose was bleeding and he felt a throbbing sensation in his forehead, just above his left eye.

Although every particle of his body was hurting, nothing seemed to be broken and he was able to sit up on the branch that was holding him. After resting for a few minutes, he patted the branch gratefully to thank it for saving his life. He then slowly climbed down the tree, wincing with pain as he went. Once on the ground, the first thing he discovered was that the front wheel of his bicycle was twisted like a beer pretzel.

As he slumped down against the bottom of the tree to wait for the pain in his leg to let up, he noticed that the earth seemed to be tilting. He closed his eyes to make the tilting stop and when he opened them again he saw Steve running towards him. There was a strange expression on his brother's face, one that Bubsy had never seen before. It was a mixture of fear and concern— but mostly fear.

"Are you all right?" Steve knelt down and grasped Bubsy's shoulder.

"Are you all right?" he asked again. There was something frantic in his voice and Bubsy saw that his big brother's eyes were clouded with tears. Yes, tears! Was this the same Steve who had just chased him all over town and forced him to go down Suicide Road?

"Can you stand up? Are you all right? Answer me, Bubsy!"

"I'm okay," Bubsy mumbled.

At this Steve breathed a sigh of relief.

I thought you were a goner," he said. "You were airborne!"

"I landed in the tree," Bubsy muttered.

Steve looked up at the broken branches that had saved his brother's life and there was amazement in his eyes. Then he noticed the bicycle.

"Your bike's wrecked," he said.

"Yeah, and it's your fault," Bubsy said accusingly.

"My fault!" Steve exploded. "Why's it my fault?! You're the one that tried to ride it down the hill, not me! I'm not responsible for your stupidity!"

"I wouldn't have done it if you hadn't been chasing me!" Bubsy countered.

"Yeah, but I wouldn't have chased you if you hadn't busted my plane—you and that dumb chimpanzee you call a friend. It's going to take me a whole week to fix it like it was!" Then, noticing that Bubsy's face was all screwed up with pain, Steve's voice softened abruptly. "Anyway Bubsy, I wasn't really going to hurt you. I was just having a little fun. So you can't say it was my fault because it wasn't. You did it all by yourself."

Bubsy realized it was useless to argue with him, so he gritted his teeth and tried to get back on his feet. But the pain in his leg became so intense that he sank down again. The concerned expression returned to Steve's face...

"I'd better go get Dad to come and pick you up," he suggested.

"I can make it home on my own," Bubsy protested. "I just need to rest for a little while."

"All right," Steve said soothingly, "Whatever you say, little brother. But I'm gonna request one small favor... When they ask you what happened, leave me out of it. Just tell them you were riding down a hill and you lost control. Because it's the truth anyway, except you don't tell them I was chasing you, that's all. If you do, they'll just get madder and it won't do you any good because I'll have to tell them you broke my airplane. So leave me out of it, okay? And I'll tell you what... If you leave me out of it, you can have your card table back. Okay?"

There was a worried, pleading look in Steve's eyes, and for just a second Bubsy actually felt a little sorry for him. Anyway, he did have a point. What good would it do to tell on him? None. So why bother? Besides, this way he'd get his card table back.

Steve saw that Bubsy was wavering, so he closed in for the kill... "And from now on there'll be no more fighting," he announced. "From now on, we're going to be real brothers. And that's a promise." He smiled warmly at Bubsy and gently patted his shoulder. "So how about it, little brother?"

"But I get my card table back, right?"

"I promise. And may the earth fall on my head if I lie," Steve said, holding his hand over his heart.

"Okay, I won't tell them," Bubsy promised.

"Great!" Steve exclaimed, again patting him on the shoulder. "I won't forget this. Not that it was my fault, but it'll save us both a lot of extra trouble."

"Yeah," Bubsy agreed.

"Now let's get you home," Steve said happily. He then tried to help Bubsy to his feet, but Bubsy pushed him away.

"I can make it by myself," he muttered as he struggled to his feet.

"All right, all right. Whatever you say. Anyway, I'll take what's left of your bike back for you," Steve said. He then picked up the mangled wreck and started up the hill. A moment later, Bubsy hobbled along after him.

"You okay?" Steve asked, looking back at him.

"Yeah, I'm okay," Bubsy mumbled. But it wasn't really true. With every step he took, the pain in his leg seemed to get worse.

"When you get home, sneak in and wash your face before Mom sees you or she'll have a fit," Steve instructed. "There's blood all over it."

A few minutes later, the pain in Bubsy's leg got so bad that he called out to his brother for help. But it was too late. Steve had disappeared over the top of the hill.

When Bubsy finally reached the top himself, several agonizing minutes later, he could not take another step. He collapsed on the ground and stared into space. His leg was killing him, his head was throbbing, his arm felt like it was on fire. Then he saw his bike lying nearby. Steve had not taken it home as he'd said he was going to.

Tears came into Bubsy's eyes as he stared at the mangled piece of junk that had once been his beloved BMX. He didn't want to cry. He was too old to cry. But then, finally, he couldn't hold back any longer. All the hurt and all the pain he was feeling flooded out of him at once. He cried. Quietly, he cried.

It wasn't just that he was hurting all over. It wasn't only because his beloved BMX was ruined. No, he cried because his whole life seemed so bleak and dismal and hopeless. No matter how hard he tried, he always came out the loser. Or so it seemed to him then, sitting alone and wounded in the dirt at the edge of the hill.

"What's the matter?" a voice gently asked him.

He looked up and dimly, through a curtain of tears, he saw someone standing a short distance away. It was a girl with a skateboard.

He blinked and her face came into view. It was a pretty face. It seemed to be a familiar face.

"Are you all right?" she asked.

He blinked again and saw it was Cathy Chung. There was a look of great concern in her dark eyes.

"I'm okay," he mumbled, wiping his face off with his hands. He tried to rise to his feet, but he staggered backwards and fell down. His legs did not seem to be working properly.

"I'll help you," she said, rushing to his side.

She assisted him to his feet and he just stood

there for a moment, trying to keep his balance.

"Can you walk?" she asked him.

"I think so," he replied. "I walked up the hill a few minutes ago."

He hobbled to his mangled bike and unsuccessfully tried to raise it up. She ran to the other side of it and helped him.

"What happened?" she asked as together they got the BMX upright.

"I tried to ride down Suicide Road," he informed her.

"You tried to ride down that hill!" she exclaimed with disbelief.

"Yeah, but I didn't make it," he said with a grim smile.

"You're crazy," she responded, shaking her head.

"I know," he agreed.

They began to make their way to his house, working together to hold the twisted front wheel off the ground so the wreck could be rolled along on its wobbly back wheel.

They didn't talk much as they went. Bubsy was still in a lot of pain and he was also a little shy of her. Cathy said almost nothing, although she

smiled encouragingly at him from time to time.

A half hour later, they carried the bike up their back alley to the garage behind Bubsy's house. She helped him get the door open and together they put the wrecked bicycle inside. Afterwards they just stood there, not saying anything but not making a move to go their separate ways, either. It was Bubsy who finally broke the silence…

"Thanks for helping me," he said.

"It's okay," she smiled. "I like crazy people. I'm a little crazy myself."

When he heard this, his aches and pains seemed to vanish for a moment and Bubsy's heart began to beat a little faster. Cathy was especially pretty when she smiled.

"I have to go now," she said after a long moment of silence.

Bubsy watched her walk up the alley to her gate. He watched her until she'd gone all the way up the back sidewalk and into her house. Then he turned reluctantly toward his own door.

He looked at the torn sleeve on his shirt and felt the bump above his left eye. He knew he must look like he'd been through a war and he knew how his mother and dad would react when they saw him. For sure they'd have a first-class parent fit and ground him for a year. But there was no use putting if off. He limped toward the door and on the way he noticed that the sky was now full of winking stars. It was strange he hadn't seen them before. In fact, he hadn't even noticed the darkness creep into place.

He opened the back door and quietly slipped inside. His hope was that he'd be able to wash himself off and change his clothes before they saw him.

"Bubsy?" his mother said from the kitchen.

He could hear her walking to the hallway. There was no way to escape.

"Where have you been? You're late! The rest of us have already eaten and—Bubsy?"

When his mother saw him, she froze on the spot and her face went all weird. Her mouth moved, but no words came out. His father also looked completely stunned when he came into the hall behind her, but at least he managed to say something.

"Are you all right, Bubsy?!" he asked with a worried frown.

"I'm okay," he said. Actually this was pretty far

from the truth, for at the moment his head was aching, his arm throbbed, and his leg felt positively numb. In fact, when he took a step towards them he almost fell over. He had to put a hand against the wall to steady himself.

His mother rushed to him and held him in her arms. "Oh Bubsy," she moaned. "You've got blood all over your face."

She was nearly in tears, so he tried to reassure her.

"I'm all right Mom," he said again. "Really. I just had a little nosebleed and I banged my arm a little bit. I fell off my bike, that's all."

They helped him into the kitchen and sat him down on a chair next to the table. Looking over at the dirty dishes, Bubsy absently noted that they'd had baked beans and a lettuce salad for supper, along with tapioca pudding for dessert. He hadn't missed much, he thought. Anyway, food didn't interest him at that moment. In fact the sight of it made him feel slightly nauseous.

While his father carefully examined Bubsy's sore leg and his wounded arm, his mother gently washed his face with a warm cloth. She made soft, cooing sounds as she dabbed away the blood.

It was as if he were a baby and she was trying to comfort him. But he didn't object because it was a special occasion for her. After all, he didn't get banged up like this every day and if it made her feel good to make those noises, that was fine with him. Actually, if he were to be perfectly honest, he had to admit that it was rather nice to hear those old, half-forgotten mother sounds again.

"Does this hurt?" his father inquired, as he gently applied a little pressure on Bubsy's elbow joint.

"OUCH!" Bubsy responded.

"What really happened to you, Bubsy?" his mother quietly asked after she'd finished with his face.

"I told you. I fell off my bike."

"You don't get like this just from falling off a bicycle," she said with a frown.

He looked at his mother and blinked. She was no dummy.

"Come on," his father said gently. "We want the truth."

Bubsy knew then that he would have to tell them the truth—or a good part of it, at least. So he looked down at the patterned vinyl floor and told them how he'd tried to ride down Suicide Road. The only important thing he didn't tell them was that he'd actually been airborne and had landed in a tree. And he didn't tell them why he'd done it. In fact he didn't mention Steve at all, because of the promise he'd made to his brother. Besides, Bubsy knew that Steve would take a terrible revenge on him if he squealed. But even while he was telling his parents about his wild ride down the hill, he knew that because he wasn't telling them the whole truth now, at the beginning, he could never tell them the rest of it later on. If he did, they would accuse him of lying because he had left Steve out of it. But it didn't matter. They'd never know. And besides, this way he'd get his card table back.

"Oh Bubsy, what are we going to do with you?" his mother said tearfully, after he'd finished his story. She shook her head sadly and looked over at Bubsy's father. Rather surprisingly, his father said nothing at all. In fact he wasn't even looking at Bubsy. He was staring up at the ceiling as if he were in some kind of trance. Then he quietly knelt down again and gave Bubsy's leg another inspection. When he'd finished, he stood up and smiled grimly at Bubsy's mother.

"I don't think there's any broken bones," he said.

"Well I'm taking him in to Emergency just to make sure," Bubsy's mother responded. "There's this bump on his forehead too," she added. "He might have a concussion. I'm taking him in right now," she said decisively.

"Yes, you're right," his father agreed.

"I don't want to go to the hospital," Bubsy protested.

Despite his protests, they quickly bundled him into the car and headed off into the night. A short time later, Bubsy found himself limping up to the Emergency entrance of the General Hospital, with a parent on each side to make sure he didn't try to escape.

"I'm really all right," he insisted for the tenth time.

"We'll let the doctor decide that," his mother informed him as she herded him through the entrance.

At the end of a long hour of waiting for a doctor, then waiting for X-rays and then waiting for the doctor again, Bubsy was informed that he had no broken bones and only a very mild concussion. He would be fine. Rest and aspirin for his headache were what Doctor Mellon prescribed for him.

When they got home from the hospital, his father asked Bubsy to come out to the garage with him. He wanted to look at the bicycle, he said.

Limping along behind him, Bubsy looked anxiously up at the cold, distant stars. What would his father say when he saw the mangled wreck that lay waiting inside the garage?

This is going to be unpleasant, he thought.

After his dad had closely examined the sorry remains of the BMX, he stood up and shook his head in dismay. Now it would finally come, Bubsy thought. The anger, the scolding…

But it didn't happen. Instead, his father put his hand gently on Bubsy's shoulder and looked down at him in a very strange way. His eyes had the most peculiar twinkle in them—as though he were about to start laughing.

"You know it really was a stupid trick to try to ride down that hill," he said at last.

"I know," Bubsy answered, swallowing hard.

"But you weren't the first to do it," his father informed him.

"I wasn't?"

"No you weren't," his father replied with a grim smile. "I did it too."

"You did?"

"Twenty-five years go. In fact I was just about your age—around eleven or twelve, I think."

"What happened to you?" Bubsy asked.

"I couldn't make that turn near the bottom," his father chuckled. "I wound up hanging from one of those trees. It saved my life."

"Mine too!" Bubsy exclaimed.

"Wrecked my bike," his father said. "Worse than yours."

"Then what happened?" Bubsy asked. He was eager to know all the details.

"What happened? What happened was your grampa spanked my backside," he said with a grin.

"You aren't going to…"

"Oh no, don't worry," his father laughed.

There was a pause while the two of them look-ed at each other and then at the badly wounded BMX.

"Don't worry about it," his father said, break-ing the silence. "We'll get you a new front wheel and fix it as good as new. First thing next spring we'll do it and that's a promise."

"Thanks, Dad!" Bubsy exclaimed.

"Now I think we'd better head back. Your steak should be about ready."

"What steak?" Bubsy asked.

"A T-bone steak."

"But I thought you had beans for supper," Bubsy said as they went up the walk.

"We did, but your mother and I thought you needed something special to help build up your strength." He smiled down at Bubsy and patted his shoulder. "And maybe I'll make you one of my super-duper chocolate sundaes for dessert," he went on. "Or would you prefer tapioca pudding?"

"No way!" Bubsy exclaimed.

After supper Bubsy limped upstairs to the bedroom. He found his brother hard at work repairing the tail on the airplane. Steve smiled at him as he came into the room. "You didn't tell them," he said in a matter-of-fact voice.

"I just told them I tried to ride down Suicide Road," Bubsy reported. "I didn't even say you were there."

"I know. I was listening," his brother said as he

calmly held a piece of balsa wood up and examined it against the light.

Bubsy went over to the closet and pulled out the box containing his Snoopy lamp and his other things. He carried it over to the table and stood there expectantly, smiling at his brother.

"Can I have my card table back now?" he asked.

"Maybe in a couple of weeks," Steve said without looking up.

"You rotten liar!" Bubsy exclaimed, after a second of stunned silence.

"I'm not the only one," his brother said with an evil grin. "You lied too. Only yours was worse."

Bubsy might have had a fit then and there, but he was too sore and tired to be able to handle it.

"I'm going to tell them what really happened," he threatened.

"Well I'd think about it, if I were you," his brother said, not in the least bothered by Bubsy's threat. Then Steve looked up with eyes so ice-cold they sent a chill through Bubsy. "Because if you do," he went on, "then they'll know you lied to them, and you know how they hate being lied to."

As Bubsy carried his box back to the closet,

Steve's low, hyena-like laughter rattled across the room. While Bubsy slowly and painfully climbed up to his bunk, the laughter went on and on.

"I'll never trust you again," Bubsy promised.

"Yes you will," Steve responded. "And do you know why? It's because you're just a little lump of sucker-bait and that's all you'll ever be."

Later on, he heard Steve getting undressed and very soon afterwards his brother was snorting peacefully in his sleep in the bunk below. As Bubsy lay there, still aching all over and with a throbbing headache that wouldn't let him sleep, he realized he had only one serious problem in his life—Steve. Steve made his life miserable. Always had, for as far back as Bubsy could remember.

Yes, all his other problems were nothing compared to the one that lay snorting down below.

But what could a little lump of sucker-bait do about him?

Nothing...Nothing...There was just no answer to Steve.

Chapter 7

When Kate opened her door the next morning, she was horrified by the wounded little creature who stood before her. Was it Bubsy?

It was Bubsy, but his left eye had a great black ring all around it. He looked like half a raccoon.

Yes, it was Bubsy alright, but his left arm was in a sling and he was tilting sideways to keep the weight off his bad leg. Kate turned white at the sight of him.

"Bubsy!" she gasped. "What happened?"

"It isn't broken," he said when he saw her eyes fasten on the sling.

"For heaven's sake come in and tell me what happened!" she exclaimed.

They sat down and he told her everything. After he'd finished, she shook her head in disbelief...

"What an awful bully he is!" she exclaimed angrily, hugging Bubsy carefully. "You could have been killed! I've a good mind to go right over there and scrunch him myself! Do your mom and dad know what he did!"

"Don't tell them!" Bubsy exclaimed excitedly.

"You mean they don't know what he did?" Kate asked with a frown.

"I didn't tell them," he confessed. "I just told them I tried to ride down the hill. So if you tell them about Steve, they'll be mad all over again because I didn't tell them all of it. And then Steve will be mad too. You can't tell them, Auntie Kate!"

"Oh Bubsy!" Kate exclaimed. "Don't you see what's going on here? Steve's tied you up with your own lie!" She looked at him and shook her head sadly. "See what happens when you don't tell the truth?"

"I know," Bubsy replied in an agonized voice. "But it's too late to tell them now. It would just make everything ten times worse."

The expression on his face was so disturbed that Kate held him again and gently patted his head.

"All right. All right. Calm down," she said soothingly. "I think you're wrong not to tell your mom and dad what really happened, but I won't say anything to them. What you tell me here is strictly between us, just like I promised. But all the same, something must be done about Steve or he'll be the death of you. The brute!"

"He pushes me around all the time!" Bubsy exclaimed. "Sometimes I can hardly stand it!"

He had to admit there were occasions, however few, when Steve was okay—for instance when they played catch together before supper. And once in a while, when Steve was in an exceptionally good mood, he gave Bubsy things. For example, when Steve got tired of collecting Batman comic books, he gave them all to him. But most of the time, Steve simply ordered Bubsy around, teased him, bawled him out, chased him away, borrowed money which he didn't pay back and otherwise lorded it over him like he was the King and Bubsy was the slave.

"He must be stopped," Kate said. "You can't go on living like this."

"I can't do anything about him," Bubsy said.

"Oh, I think the problem has a solution somewhere," she said confidently. "You just have to find it, that's all."

Bubsy shook his head. "I could never beat

him," he said. "He always wins in the end."

"Well, I don't want to interfere," she replied, "but just let me tell you a little story."

"A story?"

"Yes, but let's have some ice-cream first. You need to build up your strength."

"Have you ever heard of Abraham Lincoln?" she asked as he limped into the kitchen behind her.

"Of course I have!" Bubsy exclaimed. "He was President of the United States during the Civil War. He freed the slaves. I know all about him."

"Of course you do," Kate laughed. "Everybody knows about Abraham Lincoln. He was one of the greatest men who ever lived."

"So?"

She handed him an ice-cream bar, then sat down across the table from him. "I was just remembering a little story he once told," she said. "One day he was ploughing a field with a mule. Everything was going along fine and then he ran into this huge stone. It was buried in the middle of the field. He tried to move it out of the way, but it was too large and heavy. So do you know what he did?"

"What?"

"He just ploughed around it," Kate replied with a gleam in her eye.

Bubsy thought for a moment and then saw the light...

"You mean if I can't do anything about Steve, I should go around him?"

"Exactly."

"Like stay out of his way?" Bubsy asked.

"Yes, like stay out of his way. Get him out of your life as much as you can."

"But I can't stay out of his way. We're in the same bedroom."

"Think about what you just said," Kate suggested.

"You mean if I had a room of my own, then I could keep out of his way?"

"You've got it," Kate nodded.

Bubsy gave her a disappointed look.

"What's the matter?" she asked. "Wouldn't you like to have a room of your own?"

Wouldn't he like to have a room of his own? The question almost made him laugh. For years he'd dreamed of having a room of his own where Steve wouldn't be able to make his life a constant misery. Oh yes, it would be heaven to have a place where he could put up his own posters and nobody would take them down, where he could put his things out instead of keeping them hidden away in cardboard boxes, where he could do his homework in peace and quiet and not have to listen to Steve's screeching music, and where he could invite his friends and Steve couldn't come along and kick them all out because he didn't want them around. A room of his own? There was nothing in the world he wanted more. And nothing he was less likely to get.

"They can't give me one because there aren't any spare rooms in the house," he said to her.

"Sure they can," Kate responded. "If they really want to, they can."

"I've asked them for my own room a hundred times," Bubsy assured her, "but they always say no. They always say there aren't any extra rooms. Sometimes they even get mad at me for asking."

"They could build an extra room onto the house," Kate suggested.

"They don't have any money for that," Bubsy quickly responded.

"Your father's a good carpenter. He could do

the work himself so it wouldn't cost that much," she said. "Besides, didn't you tell me they're planning to buy a newer car next year?"

"Yes, but…"

"Well, they don't need a newer car," Kate declared. "They can spend the money on your room instead." She smiled at him. "What I mean is, they don't need another car as much as you need a room of your own."

Bubsy nodded at her. Now that was true. That was so true. But there was still the problem of making them realize it. He shook his head at his aunt. "They wouldn't do it," he said flatly. "Even if I asked them a hundred more times, they'd still say no."

"You should try to think positively," Kate smiled, patting his hand. "Ask yourself what would make them do it."

Bubsy thought about it, but he had no answer.

"Really put yourself in their shoes," Kate suggested. "Imagine you're them and you've got two sons who share a room. What would make you give your younger son a room of his own?"

After some deep thinking, Bubsy came up with a possible answer…

"I guess if they were always fighting with each other, then I'd get tired of listening to it," he said at last. "And if I couldn't make them stop, the only answer would be to give them separate rooms."

"That's it exactly," Kate said. "You see! There is a solution!"

"But Steve and I already fight all the time," Bubsy pointed out.

"Yes, but do they realize it?" Kate asked him. "From what you've told me, Steve is careful to bully you in a quiet way so they won't know what's really going on up there in that room."

Bubsy suddenly understood everything. It wasn't enough to simply fight with Steve, it was also necessary to get his parents involved in the squabbles. Then they'd get tired of the constant bickering and they'd have to do something to stop it. And what could they do? Only one thing. Give him a room of his own.

Kate saw that he understood and she smiled at him. "Mind, I don't want to interfere," she said quietly, putting her hands on her knee and staring innocently down at the floor. "It's all your idea and it's entirely up to you what you decide to do with it."

As Bubsy thought about it, the idea seemed to get better and better. It could work. It definitely could.

He knew there was one more thing he would have to do to make his plan succeed. In the fights with Steve, he would have to make sure that his brother was always in the wrong. That way his parents would feel sorry for their poor little Bubsy and they'd be much more likely to give in and build him a room of his own.

Yes, he was positive of it. Fighting with Steve and getting his mother and dad involved in the squabbles was the way for him to get a room of his own.

Now the idea really took possession of him. His eyes positively glimmered with excitement as he thought about it.

The fights couldn't be over big things. After all, he didn't want to make his brother too mad. That would be dangerous. What was needed were small squabbles. But they had to be loud. And the sillier, the better. His instinct told him it was silly little squabbles that would really get under his parents' skin and set them thinking in the right direction.

"I'm going to do it!" he exclaimed with youthful determination.

"I do believe you are," Kate said with a laugh. "But I'd advise you not to mention having a room of your own while all this is going on. Let your mom and dad figure it out for themselves."

"Why?" he asked.

"Because they're much more likely to give you a room if they think it's their own idea. People don't like to be pressured into things."

"Yes, that's right!" Bubsy agreed enthusiastically.

She patted his hand firmly and smiled at him. "Yes," she said confidently, "this is going to make a big difference in your life."

"It will," Bubsy happily agreed. "It will!"

When he left for home, he was full of excitement and confidence. The plan could not fail. And when it succeeded…oh, then how wonderful life would be! A room of his own. A room of his own! It would be the answer to all his prayers.

All that was needed to get things started was to think up some little thing he could do to annoy Steve—something that would get his parents involved in the resulting fight.

As Bubsy limped around the corner of Belfast

Street, he suddenly had an idea. Maybe it wasn't the greatest idea in the world, but it would be good enough to begin the hostilities. He was very anxious to get the ball rolling.

Later that night, when it was time for him to go to bed, Bubsy found Steve already asleep, snorting peacefully. He quietly picked up his brother's sneakers and put them in the bottom drawer of the desk.

Yes, it was no big deal. It wasn't exactly a brilliant trick. But at least it was a start. Just getting up enough nerve to try it was a major accomplishment. In all his life, Bubsy had never before deliberately set out to annoy his brother. Until now.

For the next hour he tossed and turned in his bed, thinking and worrying, worrying and thinking... Once he almost climbed down from his bunk to put the sneakers back where they came from. But he didn't. He had started down a new road in his life and he was determined to see where it would take him.

When Bubsy awoke in the morning , Steve was down on the floor on his hands and knees, rooting around under the bottom bunk. His rump was sticking out and Bubsy was sorely tempted to kick it.

"Have you seen my sneakers, Bubsy?" Steve asked as he stood up and looked around the room with a puzzled expression on his face.

Bubsy didn't reply. In fact, he ignored his brother entirely. He calmly went over to the chair and began to dress.

"Bubsy!" his brother shouted. "Where are my sneakers!"

He hadn't intended to tell him where they were, but his lips suddenly turned into cowards and gave the game away...

"Maybe they're in the desk," his lips suggested.

And sure enough, that's where they were.

"You put them in there, didn't you?" Steve said angrily.

"I don't know what you're talking about," Bubsy replied nervously as he quickly left the room.

On the way downstairs he was full of regret that he'd given in so easily. The plan had been to let Steve get very angry looking for the sneakers. Then, when Steve finally found them, Bubsy was going to deny that he'd hidden them—and the fight would have been on. But now there would be no fight. He'd spoiled everything by opening his mouth too soon.

A few minutes later, everyone except Steve was seated around the table, waiting for Beth to serve the breakfast. It was her turn to make it, and she always cooked scrambled eggs and bacon.

"Bubsy hid my sneakers in the desk," Steve complained as he came into the kitchen.

Suddenly an idea that might excuse his strange action popped into Bubsy's head...

"Maybe I did put them in there," he admitted. "But I had a good reason."

"What reason?" his mother asked with a frown.

"Because they stink," Bubsy said boldly. He wondered if they'd really believe that was why he'd done it. Probably not.

"He's gone crazy!" Steve shouted.

"Bubsy's right," Beth suddenly proclaimed. "Steve's feet smell awful! The other night when we were watching TV, he put them on the sofa and I could smell them. It made me want to throw up."

Bubsy smiled at his sister. He hadn't expected this kind of support—least of all from her.

"Maybe it wouldn't hurt if you ran your sneakers through a cycle in the washer," his father suggested.

"You haven't got a touch of Athlete's Foot, have you?" his mother asked him worriedly.

"There's nothing wrong with my feet!" Steve exclaimed.

"Except they stink," Beth persisted.

"Just to be on the safe side, you'd better put your sneakers through the washer tonight," his father said.

"Steve, I want to take a close look at your feet when you come home," his mother announced. "After you've taken a shower," she added.

Bubsy smiled happily as he watched his brother squirm under the general attack against his feet. He had not expected all this unasked-for support —especially since Steve's feet didn't really stink that much.

"They don't stink! My feet have never stunk!" Steve protested. But a worried look had crept into his eyes.

"You can't tell if your own feet stink," Beth pointed out. "Only other people can tell."

"Maybe you should start using some kind of foot powder," his mother suggested. "Or maybe we should get you some kind of special cleansing cream. It might help."

When Bubsy arrived home from school that afternoon, Steve's sneakers were hanging on the clothesline. Steve himself was upstairs in the room, repairing the tail on his model. Underneath the card table, his feet were sitting inside two large, pink, plastic buckets. Bubsy stared at the strange sight until Steve looked up at him with a worried glance...

"My coach at school says if you soak your feet once a day in baking soda and cold water, they won't stink."

Chapter 8

That night after school, Bubsy went up to the bedroom to think things over. Although the sneaker attack had turned out very satisfactorily in a way, he knew it hadn't helped him much toward getting his own room. What he needed was a fight where his brother would definitely be in the wrong. But what?

At first nothing came to mind, but when he was getting one of his Peanuts books from his box in the closet, he finally hit on an idea that could work.

As might be expected, Steve's clothes occupied nearly all the available closet space. Bubsy's clothes were all squashed together on the far right of the closet rod. And Steve was very particular about Bubsy keeping his clothes only on his small part of the rod. If he accidently hung something over in Steve's area, his brother would simply dump it on the floor.

As Bubsy looked at Steve's clothes hanging there, he decided he had found just the kind of squabble he'd been looking for. He immediately went into action and moved all his clothes onto Steve's part of the closet rod. He even mixed them right in with Steve's clothes, which was something his brother especially hated.

The plan worked perfectly. Later that evening, when Steve looked in the closet and discovered Bubsy's clothes in his space, he lifted the offending articles off the rod, hangers and all, and dropped them on the floor. When Bubsy came back to the room and saw the mess, he let out a series of shrill shrieks. Seconds later, his mother came running up the stairs.

"What on earth is the matter?" she asked.

He did not reply. He just stood there, staring at his clothes where they lay on the floor of the closet. When his mother came over and saw the mess, she was furious.

"What are your clean clothes doing on the floor!" she exclaimed angrily.

"I don't know," Bubsy said in his most innocent voice.

"Did Steve do this?!" she demanded.

"I didn't see him do it," Bubsy said quietly.

He followed her down to the basement, where Steve was watching TV.

"Did you throw your brother's clothes on the floor?" she asked him.

"Well, he hung them on my side of the closet," Steve explained defensively.

"You get upstairs and hang those clothes up! And don't you ever do that again!" she exclaimed in a harsh voice. "If you ever do, you'll be one sorry boy!"

"You little squealer," Steve hissed at him as soon as she'd left.

"I didn't tell her," Bubsy protested. "She saw it all by herself."

Late that night, when he was lying in bed, Bubsy felt a warm glow of contentment. The great bedroom plan was underway and it was working perfectly. Now all he had to do was to make sure that the squabbling and fighting went on and on and on. Then, sooner or later, his parents would have to separate him from Steve. They would have to give him a room of his own. What else could they do?

Bubsy almost laughed out loud in the dark as he remembered how angry his mother had been. Yes, it had all worked out perfectly, and it gave him a sense of power to be in control of things for a change. But it was only the beginning. Before he was through, Steve wouldn't know whether he was coming or going.

Just as he was drifting contentedly off to sleep, still thinking about how successfully he'd outwitted his brother, a tremendous force from below lifted him and his mattress high in the air. And as soon as he came down, it happened again. This time the force was so great it sent Bubsy right up to the ceiling and bounced him off it. From down below Steve's powerful legs were kicking up against Bubsy's mattress with all the force they could muster.

Bubsy could feel his teeth rattling in his head, so great was his impact with the ceiling. Again and again it happened, while he tried desperately to prevent himself from being battered to death by the ceiling on the way up and from falling off the bunk when he came down. The pain in his wounded leg came back with a vengeance.

"Help! Help!" he cried.

Now the upward thrusts were all coming from the wall side and Bubsy was sure he was going to be kicked off the bunk. This could mean a real broken arm. Or maybe an early death.

The kicking stopped the instant the light came on, which was just in the nick of time.

"What's going on in here?" his father asked sleepily.

"He was making me bounce!" Bubsy exclaimed, wincing with pain. "I almost fell off."

"I was just giving him a free horsey ride," Steve said lightly. "He wasn't going to fall. He's just a crybaby."

His father looked down at Steve and frowned. "Stop making him bounce and get to sleep," he said.

After his father had gone, Bubsy lay still as a wounded bird while he waited for his heartbeat to return to normal.

"Next time you die," Steve hissed from below.

The next day after school, Bubsy visited Kate and told her how well the closet plan had worked. He also told her about the severe bouncing he'd received from his brother in return.

"He's got less imagination than I thought," she

commented. "But the main thing is, it worked. It got both your mother and your father involved and you came out the good guy. It's exactly the sort of thing you want."

"But I can't think of what to do next," he admitted.

"I really mustn't interfere darling, but one might suggest you try to think of some little thing that especially annoys him," Kate suggested. "It might give you another idea."

"Well he doesn't like anything in our room to be messy," Bubsy said. "He likes everything to be put away in its place. He's a real 'neat freak'."

"That's interesting," Kate nodded. "You might be able to do something with that."

"Whenever I have to put on clean clothes, he makes me take the dirty ones to the laundry basket right away," Bubsy went on. "He really hates it if I ever leave them lying around near his bunk. He's afraid of my germs."

There was a long pause, then a smile spread across Bubsy's face…

"I think I've got an idea," he said.

"Good. Let's hear it," Kate responded enthusiastically. "Only as a matter of interest," she added more calmly, "since I'm not involved in any way."

He explained the idea to her and she found it highly amusing and very original. He even thought of a name for it. He called it "The Dirty Shorts Attack".

"I like it," Kate said. "I like it a lot."

They chatted about his idea for his next fight with Steve until it was time for him to go home for supper. As he was leaving , he hesitated at the door and then turned back to her…

"Maybe I should wait a while before I do it," he said. "If we have too many fights all at once, Mom and Dad might get suspicious."

"You really are a cunning little devil!" Kate laughed. "But you're absolutely right. It's best not to overdo it. Things like this take time."

"I'll come over tomorrow," he said as he stepped out.

"Tomorrow I'm going up north to see some theatre people," she said.

"When are you coming back?" he asked.

"I'll be back a week from Friday. Come and see me then."

A few days later, Bubsy came home from school and went up to the bedroom. The day of The

Dirty Shorts Attack had come. He'd made up his mind. Tonight at bedtime he would do it.

He started to throw his backpack on the card table as he always used to do, but caught himself just in time. He stared down at the giant balsa wood model with its new tail while he waited for his breath to come back. That was a close call.

As he gazed down at the huge airplane, it suddenly occurred to him that Steve's taking over his card table was also a very good excuse for a major argument. In fact, it was perfect. It was even better than The Dirty Shorts Attack. Best of all, it was an argument where he would be absolutely in the right. Everyone knew the card table was his, and Steve had no right to take it away. The idea was so excellent that he decided not to wait. He would do it right now. This very minute.

He put his backpack on the floor, then gently lifted the huge model and carefully carried it over to Steve's desk. He smiled to himself. As soon as Steve saw that he'd moved it, the fight would be on. And Bubsy knew it was a fight he couldn't lose.

Unfortunately, the desk was cluttered with Steve's books and when Bubsy put the plane down on top of them, it started to tip. He moved quickly to stop it from falling over. Too quickly. His hand accidentally struck one of the wings and it broke away from the body of the airplane.

"Oh no," he moaned.

All thoughts of dirty tricks, all thoughts about getting his own room instantly vanished as he stared in horror at what he'd done.

With trembling fingers, he carefully picked up the airplane and placed it on the card table exactly where it had been. He gently put the wing beside it, then made himself scarce.

After supper, Steve went up to their room and Bubsy waited for the screams to start. But there was nothing, only an eerie silence. Eventually, overcome with curiosity, he went upstairs and peeked into the room. Steve was sitting at the desk with his feet in the pink buckets. He was staring out the window. There was no expression on his face. None.

"It was an accident, Steve," Bubsy said in a small voice.

There was no response.

"I didn't mean to do it. Honestly. It was an accident!" he said again.

Steve turned slowly around and looked at Bubsy.

"It's okay," he said.

"Really?" Bubsy asked. He was stunned by his brother's calm response.

"Well, you said it was an accident," Steve murmured as he turned back to the window.

"It was," Bubsy confirmed. "It really was!"

"I believe you," Steve said quietly. "You wouldn't hurt it on purpose. You're not that stupid. So let's just forget about it."

Bubsy was very surprised by his brother's reaction. It just wasn't like him. He'd expected to be torn limb from limb. What's more, over the next few days his big brother seemed to change. He hardly bothered Bubsy at all. And, in gratitude, Bubsy abandoned The Dirty Shorts Attack—at least for a while.

As time passed, Steve became downright friendly. On Wednesday after school, Bubsy was in the back yard looking at the goldfish swimming around in their pond, when Steve came out of the house with his football.

"Let's throw the old pigskin around till supper," he said with a friendly smile.

"Okay," Bubsy eagerly agreed. He was anxious to please this new version of Steve.

They tossed the football back and forth for a while, until suddenly Steve stopped and pointed toward the far side of the yard.

"I just saw a snake go into the pond," he said.

They went over and looked down into the water, but Bubsy couldn't spot the snake. He stood on the concrete rim of the pond and looked all over, but he still couldn't see it.

"Do garter snakes go into water a lot?" he asked his brother.

Suddenly there was a terrific whump, as the football thudded lengthways against Bubsy's back. So great was the force of the impact that it hurled him forward and, since he was standing on the rim of the pond, there was only one place for him to go.

Sputtering and coughing, he raised himself out of the water. Though he couldn't see it, there was a lily pad sitting on his head. He did see his big brother grinning down at him with glittering eyes.

"Did you catch the snake?" Steve asked. Then he burst into a hideous explosion of hyena-like laughter.

"Now you're in for it!" Bubsy sputtered.

Steve looked down at his little brother sitting in the water and smiled calmly.

"It was an accident," he said.

And they believed him too.

"I just threw the football to him. It's not my fault he wasn't paying attention," Steve said to his parents a few minutes later, his voice heavy with regret.

"Go take a shower and put on some dry clothes," his mother said to Bubsy. "And after this don't stand near the pond when you're playing football."

When Bubsy came back from the shower, his brother was at the card table, soaking his feet in the pink buckets while he worked on his model. The wing was back in place.

"Do garter snakes go into water?" Steve asked in a mockingly childish voice. Then he chortled to himself for the next five minutes.

Bubsy decided then and there that The Dirty Shorts Attack would take place that night.

Chapter 9

When Bubsy went upstairs to bed that night, Steve was nowhere in sight. Perfect. Bubsy immediately changed into his pajamas, then carefully dropped his dirty T-shirt, socks and undershorts onto his brother's pillow.

Yes, it was only a small trick, but it was just the kind of thing that would make his brother blow up and, hopefully, loudly complain to their parents.

Bubsy could imagine Steve—indeed, he could almost hear him—shouting the terrible accusation across the breakfast table.

"He put his dirty, filthy underclothes on my pillow!"

"They weren't dirty. I only wore them once," Bubsy could picture himself calmly saying in reply.

The next morning when he awoke, Steve was

already up and gone. And so were the T-shirt, socks and shorts. He had expected to find them somewhere on the far side of the room, where Steve was most likely to throw germ-laden under-things, but they were not there. Nor anywhere else. They had vanished.

No problem. He simply went to the bottom drawer of the dresser for replacements. However, although he found plenty of T-shirts and socks in the drawer, there were no shorts. Yet he was positive there'd been lots of shorts in there the day before.

He found everybody downstairs eating break-fast.

"You're late this morning," his father remarked. "You'd better get a move on."

"Steve stole my shorts," he solemnly reported.

"I did not!" Steve exclaimed. His mouth was full of toast, and after he'd spoken he opened it wide so Bubsy would see what was inside. But only Bubsy.

"Why would Steve steal your shorts?" his mother asked with a laugh.

"He's capable of anything," Beth put in.

"You keep out of this," Mrs. McGourlic said to

her. Then she looked at Bubsy and frowned. "I know there's shorts in your drawer. Did you look hard?"

"I looked all over. They're gone," Bubsy insisted. "Steve stole them!"

"I didn't!" Steve exclaimed with an air of injured innocence. He opened his toast-filled mouth to Bubsy again, but this time his father saw it.

"Chew with your mouth closed," his father ordered.

"Is he doing that again!" Beth exclaimed. She threw a disgusted glance at Steve. "Sometimes you make me sick. You're such a slob!"

"I'd rather be a slob than a beetle like you," Steve muttered.

"Did you hear that!" Beth shrieked. "He called me a beetle!"

"Now don't you two start," Mrs. McGourlic warned them.

"I wasn't starting anything," Beth protested. "It's just that he's such a foul beast."

"She always picks on me," Steve complained. "Like she's the Duchess of York or something, with her snotty nose in the air."

"At least my feet don't stink," Beth said with a quiet air of superiority.

"My feet don't stink anymore!" Steve exclaimed with extreme agitation. "I soak them in baking soda every day!"

"What about my shorts!" Bubsy hollered.

"Bubsy!" his father shouted.

All was quiet for a moment, then his mother spoke.

"Everybody calm down," she said. She looked at Bubsy, still dressed in his pajamas. He was standing at the opposite end of the table with an expression of extreme distress on his face. "Wear the ones you wore yesterday," she said.

"I can't find them either," Bubsy moaned. "He stole them too."

"But I didn't," Steve protested with great sincerity. Then he looked directly at Bubsy. "Why would I steal your stupid shorts?" he asked.

For this Bubsy had no good answer. At least none that he could offer them without revealing his own nasty little trick.

"I'm really getting rather tired of this," Mrs. McGourlic sighed. "Go down to the laundry room and find a pair for today. We'll get you some clean ones tomorrow. Now hurry up or you'll be late for school."

Why hadn't he thought of the laundry room before, he wondered as he leaped down the stairs. He rushed into the room and saw several large piles of dirty clothes on the floor. It was Beth's week to do the laundry and she always put it off as long as she could, because she hated doing it.

He found lots of his socks, T-shirts, shirts and jeans, but no shorts. Note one pair! None! He ran back upstairs in a state of total panic.

"There aren't any!" he cried.

"Well I don't know what's going on!" his mother exclaimed. "You've got at least a dozen pairs of undershorts. I know you have. We just bought you six pairs last summer."

"You're going to be late for school," Beth commented as she got up from the table.

"You'd better go get dressed as best you can, or you really will be late," his mother said to him. "Because you aren't leaving here without breakfast."

On hearing her words, he felt faint with anxiety.

"I can't go to school without shorts on!" he cried out, horrified at the prospect.

"Excuse me," Steve said, dabbing his mouth with his napkin. "I'd better get going. I don't want to be late." He grinned at Bubsy as he stood up.

"Where did you hide them, Steve?" his father asked quietly.

Everyone looked at Steve.

"Well he put his dirty shorts and things on my pillow last night," Steve said defensively. "They're full of germs, you know."

"Where?" his father demanded.

"They're out in the garage," Steve confessed. "In Grampa's old tin trunk."

Bubsy did not wait to hear anything more. He raced outside and was halfway to the garage before he realized he was still in his pajamas. Unfortunately, they were the ones with the teddy bears and drums all over them that his grandmother had given him as a joke. At least he thought it was a joke.

Across the way, Cathy Chung was wheeling her bicycle into the back alley. When she saw him rushing up the sidewalk in his babyish pajamas, she burst into laughter. He didn't care. His only concern at that moment was to have shorts again.

When he was on the way back, his arms laden with underwear, Steve passed him on the sidewalk.

"Let this be a lesson to you, Nerdface," his brother chortled as he went by.

Later, as Bubsy waited for a late slip outside the Vice-Principal's office, he thought maybe he'd played enough dirty tricks on his brother for awhile.

Chapter 10

When his aunt Kate returned the following Friday, Bubsy told her about all the dreadful things that had happened to him while she was away—in particular, about how he'd gone for an unscheduled swim in the fish pond and about how horribly the Dirty Shorts Trick had backfired on him.

"He hid your shorts?" she asked with disbelief.

"In the garage," he answered. "He even hid my dirty ones. I was late for school."

While she was laughing, he looked glumly at the ceiling.

"I'm afraid to play any more dirty tricks on him," he confessed. "His are worse than mine."

"I think I'll have to agree with you," his aunt admitted.

"But I'm still not going to give up," Bubsy vowed. "Only I wish there was some way to speed things along."

They chatted for along time and the ideas began to flow freely. By the time he was ready to go home for supper, he had even thought up a clever little four-step plan. The plan was a little complicated, but he was sure it would do the trick. It would get him his bedroom and it would get it soon.

"I really think it'll work," he said confidently.

"I do too," Kate agreed. "Especially if you have a good idea beforehand what you're going to say to them."

"But I don't know what I'm going to say," Bubsy confessed.

"Then let's practice. We just pretend everything is actually happening exactly like you've planned it. Then we simply say whatever seems right and natural. You speak for yourself and I'll speak for everybody else," Kate said earnestly.

"I don't know if I can do it," Bubsy admitted.

"Come on, it's not hard. It'll be fun. In the theatre it's what we call improvisation. So why don't you come back after supper and we can work on it. Then when the time comes, you'll really be ready for them."

Bubsy agreed to give her suggestion a try and

then he headed home for supper. An hour later he was back, ready to go to work.

"Let's start with step two of your plan," Kate suggested. "I'll pretend I'm your mother and you come to me and ask the big question."

They began to play the improvisation game and Bubsy found that he liked it. The time seemed to fly by as they rehearsed all the things he would have to say and do to carry out his great plan. Finally it was time for him to go home and get a good night's sleep. The final push for the bedroom would begin tomorrow morning.

"Just let me see your sad face once more," Kate requested.

Bubsy made his sad face and Kate smiled at him. "It's very good," she said. "But remember to stick your lower lip out just a little more and let the corners of your mouth droop. It'll help if you can think of something depressing."

Bubsy suddenly looked so sad that Kate burst into laughter.

"Perfect!: she said. "You're quite a little actor, darling! You look just like a hung dog."

"I was thinking about the time my hamster died," he confessed.

Kate laughed at him again. "Okay, I think you're as ready as you'll ever be," she said.

Bubsy smiled at her and nodded.

"Now remember," she went on, "this is all your idea. Not a word about me. I wouldn't want them to think I'm interfering with your life."

As he limped off through the darkness, Bubsy felt the coolness of the October night against his face. The crispness of the air reminded him that winter was coming. In a month or so the city would be covered with snow. He wasn't looking forward to it. He disliked winter—except for playing hockey. He'd already decided that when he grew up he'd live somewhere out on the West Coast, where the grass was green all year long and everybody was happy.

As he walked around to the back door of the house, he thought about the next day. Tomorrow he would set the master plan in motion.

That night he dreamed he had a room of his own. It was large and bright, with two big windows. Along one wall was a huge closet and against another was a wide bed with two thick mattresses. There was also a huge desk, a shining dresser, and a red bookcase with all his beloved books sitting on its sturdy shelves. The walls were covered with posters—his posters. And in the middle of them all, in the place of honour, was the faithful Saint Bernard!

But by far the best thing about the room was that there was not a trace of Steve anywhere in it.

When Bubsy woke up, the first thing he saw was Steve's giant airplane model sitting on the card table. So it was all just a dream. But soon it would be real. Soon he would really have his own room.

It was Saturday morning, so he had to fix his own breakfast. After he'd eaten a bowl of cereal, he waited until Steve left the house, then ran to the garage and returned with a box of his old Matchbox toys. These were small steel trucks, cars, buses and other miniature vehicles that his grandmother had given him when he was little. He carried the box of tiny steel toys to the bedroom and scattered them all over the floor. Step one of the plan was now underway. It would be completed when Steve returned and created a fuss.

He was now ready to go ahead with step two of the master plan.

He went down to the basement and found his mother hard at work in her art room. She was completing her latest painting. This one looked like a rainbow with a bad case of diarrhea.

"Hi, Bubsy. What's on for today?" she asked with a smile.

He went over to her with a very serious expression on his face, ready to mount the direct attack he and Kate had so carefully rehearsed.

"Mother, can I have a room of my own? I don't like sharing with Steve. He oppresses me."

She laughed at him.

"How did you ever come up with a word like oppresses?"

"Well, he does! He bosses me around and he hogs the whole room."

His mother stopped painting and regarded him with a serious expression.

"We'd love for you to have a bedroom of your own," she said gently. "As a matter-of-fact, your father and I were just talking about it the other day."

"Were you?" he asked, his heart beating rapidly.

"Yes, but I'm afraid there isn't one to give you. So you'll just have to wait a few years until Beth goes to college and then you can have hers. Or Steve can have it and you can have the one you're in."

"I can't wait that long," he moaned. "I'm dying from oppression."

"Sorry, you're just going to have to stay oppressed for a while longer," she said. "There simply isn't another empty room in the house."

She turned back to her painting.

"I could have this room," he suggested.

"What?? Don't be silly. This is my studio!"

"I need it more than you do," he said boldly.

"Bubsy, what's got into you?"

"I want it," he said firmly.

"Well, you're not getting it and that's that!" she said angrily. "This is my room!"

"But you've got yours and Dad's bedroom," he pointed out.

"Yes, but I need a special room for my art work and this is it. And I'm keeping it too!" she exclaimed.

Bubsy then put on the saddest expression he'd ever worn in his whole life. Inspired by the memory of Ernest, his dead hamster, tears like small diamonds appeared in the corners of his eyes.

"Mother…"

When she turned and saw the expression on his face, with the two gleaming droplets hanging precariously from his lashes, her own eyes immediately welled up with tears. He then said the magic words he and Kate had so carefully rehearsed the night before.

"Don't you love me?" he asked her.

She hugged him and kissed him.

"Of course I love you, Bubsy. But darling, you can't have my art studio and that's all there is to it. I'm sorry."

He left her with a very clouded look in her eyes and headed upstairs to his father's office. Step two of the final attack had been successfully carried out. Everything was going according to plan. Now for step three.

His father was behind his big desk, writing something on his computer.

"Dad?"

"What is it, Bubsy? I'm very busy. I have to get this article finished for Owl Magazine."

"Could I have my own bedroom? I don't like sharing a room with Steve. He oppresses me."

His father looked up at him and smiled. "He

115

oppresses you? Where'd you get a hold of a word like that?"

"He does. He hogs the whole room and he bosses me around," Bubsy answered.

"Then I'll tell him to be nice to you," his father said. "Is that all?"

"But I need my own room," Bubsy persisted. "I need privacy. I need my own personal space."

His father gave him a searching look. "Have you been talking to your aunt Kate?" he asked.

"All I need is my own room," Bubsy said quickly, "then I'll be happy for the rest of my life."

"I seriously doubt it," his father replied. "Anyway, you're out of luck. There isn't an extra room in the house. Maybe in a few years, when Beth goes away to college."

"I can't wait that long!" Bubsy exclaimed.

"Well, you're going to have to," his father said. He turned back to his computer.

"Why can't I have this room?" Bubsy asked.

"Don't be silly," his father replied without looking up.

"I need it more than you do," Bubsy said with a blink.

"What?"

"I need it more than you do," he repeated.

"Get out of here," his father said with a laugh.

"I do," Bubsy persisted.

"Look buddy—or whatever your name is—I do my writing in this room. My writing and your mother's art are what gets us the money to buy groceries with. Now do you want to go on eating, or do you want your own room?"

"I want my own room," Bubsy said with decision.

"Well you aren't getting it," his father responded. "Now scram."

Bubsy then stuck out his lower lip and made a wonderfully sad expression appear on his face. Just the thought of the way he must look brought tears to his eyes.

"Dad," he said. His father looked up at him, but he did not seem to be moved by the sight of Bubsy's terrible suffering. He only stared at him with a puzzled expression.

"Don't you love me?" Bubsy asked with all the sorrow he could muster.

"Who've you been taking acting lessons from?" his father laughed. "Your aunt Kate?"

When his father went back to work on his computer, he was chuckling to himself.

Bubsy had a strong feeling that step three had just failed. But it didn't matter. The rest of the new bedroom plan could yet work. He still had step one to complete and step four to carry out.

Just as he turned to leave his father's den, there was a terrible scream from upstairs.

"Aahhh! Aaahhh!" And then again, even louder—"Ahhhhhh! Aahhhhhhh!" Steve was back.

His father rushed up the stairs and Bubsy ran up behind him. It seemed that step one was going to work even better than anticipated. To get his parents involved in one last squabble, Bubsy had planned to provoke Steve by absolutely refusing to pick the Matchbox toys up. But, with the way Steve was hollering his head off, that was now quite unnecessary. What's more, his mother was racing up the stairs behind them. No doubt about it, everything was going his way.

When they got to the top of the stairs, Beth was already in the hallway. She was standing outside the boys' bedroom door, from whence the screams were coming.

"Aahhhhhhhhh!!! Ahhhhhhhhh!"

"What on earth is it?" his mother gasped.

"I don't know," Beth said. "I'm afraid to open

the door."

His mother rushed to the door and opened it.

"Steve! What's the matter?" she cried.

The sight that greeted their eyes was quite strange. Steve was sitting on the floor, holding his right foot in his hand. There was an expression of intense pain on his face.

"I stepped on one of his stupid toys!" he shouted. Then he moaned loudly. "I think I broke my foot."

It turned out that Steve's foot wasn't badly broken. The X-rays at the clinic showed that only a small bone was cracked. And, on the positive side, the doctor did comment on how clean Steve's feet were. However, on the negative side, Bubsy's mother and father were very angry. They blamed him for Steve's accident. And so did Steve.

Later in the day, when Bubsy could no longer bear his brother's hostile looks, he went over to his aunt Kate's. While he was eating some cookies, he told her about how the plan had worked so far.

When he was finished, she looked at him with concern. "Steve isn't really seriously hurt, is he?"

"No, it was just a little bone that broke," Bubsy

replied. "But he has to wear a big cast on his foot. And does he ever hate it!"

"It's too bad, but maybe it'll teach him to stop bullying you," she said. "Anyway, it should help you a lot. Every time they see his cast, it'll remind them of the room problem. That's exactly what you want."

"I'm going to try step four tomorrow," he said.

"Along with everything else, it should do the trick," Kate predicted.

"It will," Bubsy said confidently. "They're almost ready to give me a room of my own. I can tell."

"Now I have to get dressed to go out," Kate said. "The Women's Action Committee is picketing City Hall today."

"Why?" he asked.

"Some of the meanies on the City Council are trying to cut back on money for the Women's Shelter," she answered.

"Can I come with you?" he asked.

"Sure. It'll make me look like a mother."

"Is that good?" he asked.

"Oh yes," she said. "Mothers with kids are very good when you're picketing for something like this."

After she'd changed into her jeans, he helped her carry the picketing signs to her truck, and they headed downtown. On the way there, she looked over at him and smiled.

"I really appreciate you helping me like this," she said. Then she put her hand on his arm. "There is one thing. The city's got a Court Injunction to try to prevent our demonstration. So if they arrest me, you go straight home."

"Okay," he said.

"And if they arrest you too, then call your mother from the police station. She'll come and get you out."

He nodded. He understood.

"Oh hey!" she exclaimed. "I just had a brilliant idea. If they do arrest you, then tell your folks you wouldn't have been with me if you'd had a room of your own to hang out in."

"I will," he promised.

Chapter 11

When they arrived at the parking lot across from City Hall, there was a large group of women waiting there. Like Kate, some of the women had brought children with them. There were also a few brave men in the crowd. That's how Kate referred to them. And what was most important to her, there was a reporter and camera person from CHAT TV positioned across the street.

Everyone rushed to the truck and grabbed picketing signs. Bubsy got one for himself. It read:

CITY HALL IS SEXIST!

He wasn't exactly sure what his sign meant, but he took it anyway.

Kate was now standing on the back of the truck with her bullhorn.

"All right everybody, if they start making arrests, join hands and sit down. And don't help them.

Let your body go limp so they'll have to carry you away."

Bubsy blinked when he saw Cathy Chung in the crowd. No, his eyes weren't deceiving him. She was really there. She had a white sweatband around her head and she looked very cool indeed. As he watched her move through the crowd with her sign held up high, his heart began to beat a little faster.

"Now let's everybody get across the street before the police arrive," Kate shouted. "And remember! When we fight for the rights of some women, we're fighting for all women!"

A loud cheer went up and the protesters began to sing We Shall Overcome as they crossed the street.

Three hours later, the demonstration was over and Bubsy was very disappointed with it. After the police had carried Kate to their van, he'd asked one of them to arrest him too. But the policeman had refused. In fact, the officer went out of his way to further insult him. He'd told Bubsy to go home and get his diapers changed.

"I hate that policeman," he said to Cathy as they walked home together.

"Which one?" Cathy asked.

"The one with the sunglasses," Bubsy replied. "I really hate him."

"I do too," Cathy said with a frown. "He told me to go home and get my diapers changed."

"Me too," Bubsy admitted.

They laughed together at their experience with the policeman, then walked on in silence until they'd gone past the Dairy Queen and started up the hill.

"I knew you had the same last name, but I didn't realize Kate was your aunt until today," Cathy said, finally breaking the silence.

"She is," Bubsy said with a touch of pride. "She's my father's sister."

"She's wonderful!" Cathy exclaimed.

"I didn't even know you knew her," Bubsy said.

"I joined the Children's Theatre as soon as we moved here," Cathy informed him. "That's where I met her."

"Oh," Bubsy said.

"She's going to direct our next play," Cathy went on. "It's called Rapunzel. It's about a princess with long hair."

"Oh yeah," Bubsy said. "I've heard of it."

124

"It's a lot of fun," she said. "I mean the Children's Theatre. Did you know about it?"

"Oh sure," Bubsy said. "I was planning to join it."

What he said was quite true, although his decision to join the theatre group was only seconds old.

"Great!" Cathy exclaimed. "We really need more boys. Can you act?"

"Sure," Bubsy said. "I've done lots of acting. My aunt gives me private lessons."

He did not mention that his acting was done at home and not in any theatre. But what did it matter? Acting is acting.

When he arrived home, the news was there before him.

"Your aunt Kate's been arrested again," his father said anxiously as Bubsy came into the kitchen. "Your mother and I are going down to try to get her out."

"If we can," his mother said. "Do you think they'll take a postdated cheque for her bail?"

"I don't think they'll ask for bail. I'll just have to sign for her like the last time," his father replied worriedly.

"She went limp, so they had to carry her to the police van," Bubsy informed them.

"How do you know?" his mother asked.

"I was there," he said. "And guess what? I'm going to be on TV!"

"From now on I want you to stay away from Kate," his father warned.

"Now Bert, you can't order him to stay away from her," his mother said. "She's his aunt and he loves her."

"Well, I don't want him to hang around her when she's doing this kind of thing," his father responded.

"Kate is always doing this kind of thing," his mother pointed out. "Anyway, I agree with her. It's time those stupid politicians started paying attention to women's needs! We should get together and throw them out of office."

"If I had my own room to hang out in, then I wouldn't have to spend so much time with Auntie Kate," Bubsy broke in.

"Blackmail isn't going to work," his father replied.

"And we've heard enough about that subject for today," his mother added. "In fact, I don't want you to mention it again. You can't have a room and that is that!"

Bubsy decided that it might be wise to wait a few days before going ahead with step four. But he was certain it would do the trick—once he got up enough nerve to try it.

A week later the first light snow fell on the city, but it was all gone by noon and the day turned sunny and warm. That same day, Bubsy's aunt appeared in court and received a small fine for her part in the demonstration. According to his parents, she really wanted to go to jail instead of paying her fine. However, the theatre needed her for their new protest play about battered women.

Bubsy stopped by her apartment on the Saturday morning after her court appearance. The experience seemed to agree with her. She was wearing a bright red silk housecoat, and was brimming over with enthusiasm for her new play. Finally he managed to get a word in…

"I'm going to try step four today," he said. "I can't wait any longer."

"Then go for it!" she urged him.

On arriving home, he made several secret trips

back and forth between the bedroom and the basement laundry room, carrying down his clothes and his cardboard boxes. After he'd fixed the laundry room up according to his plan, he sat down and began to read a book about the theatre that Kate had lent him. He didn't come out again, not even when he heard his father calling him for lunch.

At about one o'clock in the afternoon, his mother opened the door of the laundry room and saw him. He was lying on a pile of dirty clothes, reading his book. All his earthly possessions were in the room with him. His Peanuts books were on the soap shelf and his shirts and trousers were hanging from a water pipe. His Snoopy lamp was on the dryer. Everything else was tucked about here and there.

"What on earth!!" She stood in the doorway and stared at the sight with a stunned expression on her face.

"Hi Mom," he said quietly, continuing to read his book.

"What in heaven's name are you doing?" she asked. "Why are your things down here?"

"I've moved into the laundry room," he ex-

plained in a matter-of-fact voice.

"You've what?"

"I've moved into the laundry room. I need my own private space."

"Your own private space? I'm getting your father!"

She returned a moment later with his father.

"He says he needs his own private space," she informed him.

"It's Kate again," his father said. He grinned down at Bubsy. "Maybe you could take over the household laundry, since you'll be in here anyway," he suggested.

"Don't be silly," his mother replied. "He can't stay in here."

"Then can I have a bedroom of my own?" he asked them.

Now they would say the magic words. Now his struggle would finally be over. His heart was beating fast as he waited for their answer.

"No, you can't have a bedroom of your own," his father said in a hard, clear voice. "And you can save yourself the trouble of trying anything else, because your little schemes aren't going to work. Now hike your things back upstairs and I don't want to hear another word on that subject. You're not getting your own room and that's the end of it!"

He had failed. All his schemes and plans... All his hard work... All the risks he'd taken... It had all come to nothing. His soul felt empty.

Yet even now, even after everything had failed, he knew he would not give up. He would start over from the beginning if he had to, but he would not give up. He couldn't give up. If he did, then he'd never be free from the tyranny of his vicious brother. But what else could he do? What else? What?

After he'd returned everything to the bedroom, Bubsy sat on the floor and stared glumly at Steve's model airplane. He still hated it with all his heart, but now he didn't dare go anywhere near it. Since the accident with Steve's foot, he had been very careful not to do anything at all to make his brother madder than he already was—if such a thing were possible.

Steve came thumping into the room and glared at him. He'd just returned from a check-up at the clinic.

"They're going to leave this stupid cast on my

foot for another week!" he cried out angrily. "I can't stand it!"

Bubsy left the room quickly and walked over to Kate's. His own leg was better. He no longer limped at all.

"Step four didn't work," he glumly informed her. "They kicked me out of the laundry room and they said I couldn't have a room of my own. And they meant it too!"

The situation seemed nearly hopeless to him. But not to Kate.

"I don't want to interfere," she said, "but I wouldn't give up just yet. All you've got to do is start annoying him again so he'll whine to them about you. Don't worry, they'll soon get tired of listening to him. It won't take long. They're very close to surrendering."

She put a snack on the table for him and smiled. "Just do a few little things like before," she suggested. "Leave some stuff lying around. Mix your clothes in with his. Things like that."

Bubsy listened to her, but he no longer felt this approach was such a good idea. It had already failed once. Besides, Steve was in a murderous mood these days.

"I'm afraid to," he said glumly. "That cast on Steve's foot drives him crazy. Sometimes he looks like he wants to strangle me. It's scary just to be around him."

"I guess I can understand the way you feel," she said.

For a long time they were silent, lost in thought. Then suddenly Bubsy turned around and there was a look of excitement in his eyes.

"I've got another idea!" he announced. "It's the best one I've had!"

"Tell me about it," she urged him.

He told her, and Kate thought it was perfect. True, it would infuriate Steve again, but it was worth the risk. This time, his parents couldn't help but see for themselves how Steve hogged the room and bullied his little brother.

Bubsy was certain his new plan would work. It would cost a little money to carry it out, but Kate agreed to finance it.

They drove all over the city, visiting one store after another. When they were finished, they had over a dozen very interesting posters tucked in back of the seat. As soon as they arrived at the apartment, Bubsy stored all his new posters in his aunt's closet. There they would stay until it was time to carry out his plan.

"This time it's going to work," Kate predicted. "You're definitely going to have a room of your own—and soon. It's a brilliant idea!"

"I know," Bubsy said proudly.

Chapter 12

Surprise was an important part of Bubsy's new plan and he couldn't do anything until everyone else was out of the house. He found it very difficult to wait, but wait he must. A whole week passed by and there was always somebody hanging around the house. But finally, on the following Friday, at noon, an opportunity arose. Steve had just returned from the clinic with a broad smile on his face.

"Look!" he exclaimed, waving his foot in the air. "NO CAST!"

Bubsy smiled at his brother's excitement. "Does your foot feel funny without it?" he asked.

"Not a bit!" Steve said happily. "No more cast … Now I can wear a shoe on it again."

"How does the foot actually feel?" his father asked.

"It's better than new! I could even run on it, if

135

I wanted to!"

"No running," his mother warned. "You take it easy on that foot for awhile."

"You know what we should do?" his father said. "We should all go to the drive-in tonight. To celebrate the recovery of Steve's foot."

"Salmon sandwiches," Steve said happily. "Make some salmon sandwiches."

"We always have salmon sandwiches," Beth complained.

"I'll make the popcorn," Mrs. McGourlic volunteered.

"I'll make the sandwiches," Beth proposed. "But they aren't going to be salmon."

"I'm not going," Bubsy informed them.

They all stared at him with disbelief.

"You love going to the drive-in," Beth said with astonishment. "What's the matter with you, anyway?"

"I don't want to go this time," he told them. "I want to work on my animal project."

"It's the last chance this year," his father warned him. "After this weekend, it shuts down for the winter."

"I don't care," Bubsy replied.

"Well, you can't go out anywhere while we're gone," his mother warned.

"I won't," Bubsy promised.

"There's something wrong with him," Steve said, looking suspiciously down at his little brother.

"No there isn't," Bubsy replied easily. "I feel great."

"You may feel great, but you've gone looney tunes," Steve said, rotating his finger in a small circle over his head.

Bubsy phoned his aunt Kate a few minutes later. "They're all going to the drive-in tonight," he informed her in a whisper.

"Good. Call me when they leave and I'll bring the posters over," she said.

Later that night, after everyone had left for the drive-in, he called her again.

"They're gone. The coast is clear," he whispered.

"Then why are you whispering?" she asked.

"I don't know," he replied.

Kate arrived a few minutes later with her arms full of his posters, and a box of thumb tacks in her pocket.

They went directly to his room—his and Steve's room—and looked around the walls at his brother's rock posters.

"I see what you mean," she said grimly.

They went to the garage and carried the step-ladder up to the bedroom. An hour later the room had been transformed.

Bubsy lay on the floor and looked up at what they'd done. Altogether, there were thirty-seven dogs up there on the ceiling. There were Beagles and Huskies, a streamlined Greyhound, a gentle Newfoundland, an angry-looking pair of Dober-man Pinschers, three Border Collies, one Giant Schnauzer, four bug-eyed Pekingese, a pack of Bloodhounds, one Old English Sheepdog (it was hard to tell which end of it was which), six Dalmatians, two great Danes, one Bulldog, a Mexican Hairless with three pups, and, staring down at him from the place of honour, was the huge Saint Bernard.

The posters covered the entire ceiling, except for the light fixture.

As he lay there and gazed up at them, Kate lay down beside him and immediately burst into laughter. "I've never seen anything like it!" she giggled.

"Steve is going to hate them," Bubsy predicted

a little nervously. "He really hates dogs."

"Then it's definitely going to work," Kate assured him. "Now when he runs to complain to your mom and dad, you make a real big fuss. Argue for all you're worth."

"I will," he promised.

"After all, fair's fair," Kate said. "And Bubsy dear, for heaven's sake don't tell them I helped you. They might accuse me of interfering."

After his aunt left, Bubsy watched TV until he heard his family coming in, then he rushed upstairs to meet them.

"You missed two good movies," Beth advised him.

"I don't care," he said. "Anyway, I finished my project."

"Well, that's nice," his mother said. "You'll have to show it to us."

"You'll see it," he promised.

"What kind of project was it?" his father asked. "Was it something for Social Studies?"

"Oh, it wasn't for school," Bubsy responded. "I just put some dog posters up, that's all."

At that exact moment, there was a terrible shriek from upstairs.

"It's just Steve," Bubsy informed them. "I don't think he likes my posters."

A second later Steve came down the stairs in a state of wild hysteria.

"Come and see what he's done to my room!" he exclaimed.

Everyone headed upstairs and into the room. They wandered around, looking up in amazement at all the dogs on the ceiling. Bubsy waited patiently for their verdict.

"But why didn't you put them on the walls?" his mother asked him.

It was the exact question he'd been waiting for...

"Because Steve wouldn't let me," he replied with a carefully prepared downcast expression. "All the posters on the walls are his. He wouldn't let me put even one of mine up."

"Is that so?" his father asked, frowning at Steve.

"Mine were there first," Steve replied uneasily.

"Then I guess you're stuck with this," his father said, waving his hand toward the postered ceiling.

"Actually, it's rather interesting," his mother decided. "All those dogs gathered together. It's like a work of art."

"This room is definitely weird," Beth commented with a shudder.

"I can't live with a dog kennel on my ceiling!" Steve shrieked.

"They're just pictures," Bubsy said calmly.

"I can't stand it!" Steve exclaimed.

"Well, you'll just have to get used to it," his father declared. "After all, it's his room too."

"You wouldn't let him put any of his posters on the walls, so it's your own fault," his mother added.

After they'd left, Steve sat down on his bunk and glared at Bubsy.

"I'll get you for this," he said in a voice that was so low and so harsh it would have frightened Conan The Barbarian.

"I've got my rights," Bubsy said defiantly. He did not appear to be frightened. In fact he deliberately looked up at his dogs and smiled broadly.

"You little wimp! You're gonna be sorry for this!" Steve hissed.

Bubsy glanced over at his scowling brother and at that moment resolved never again to let himself be pushed around. He would fight back until the death, if necessary—although he did hope it wouldn't be necessary.

Anyone who knew Bubsy, and saw the defiant expression on his face right then, would realize that there was something very different about him. Perhaps it was the calm, determined look in his eye. Whatever it was, they would take one glance and know that this wasn't the nice, quiet, easily-managed little Bubsy they were used to. Something basic in his nature had changed that made this new Bubsy seem bigger and harder and more confident than the old one.

Exactly how Bubsy's amazing transformation had occurred might not be easily explained, but the important thing was that he wasn't afraid of his bullying brother anymore. Yes, whether Bubsy got his own room or not, things were going to be different from now on.

"I want my card table back," he said quietly.

"I told you, you little wimp! When I've finished my model, you'll get it back. In the meantime you can get those stupid posters off my ceiling."

"I want my card table," Bubsy insisted, ignoring his brother's order. There was that same quiet, determined look in his eye as he spoke.

"Are you nuts? You want to get pounded?" Steve shrieked.

"If you don't get your model off my card table, I'm going to move it myself," Bubsy said, ignoring his brother's threat.

"All right, you asked for it!" Steve yelled, leaping to his feet. As he spoke, he raised his bony fist in a threatening manner.

Bubsy did not flinch or run from him, as he had done so often in the past. This time he stood his ground and looked his brother directly in the eye...

"If you hit me, I'm going to hit you back," he promised. "Then there's going to be a fight and I'm going to get hurt because you're bigger and then they'll see what a bully you are and you're the one who'll be sorry."

All this he said boldly and without stopping for a breath.

Steve looked at him with amazement. What was going on? All at once this little rat was becoming extremely difficult to handle—and a major irritation, as well. He wasn't at all like the old Bubsy. Worst of all, Steve wasn't quite sure what he should or could do about it. He lowered his fist and a very puzzled expression appeared on his face.

"Now get your stupid model off my card table," Bubsy said with a sneer. He sensed that victory was in the air, waiting to be seized. But, unfortunately, he was reaching a little too far for it. One thing for certain. He should not have sneered at Steve.

The idea that Bubsy would dare to defy him was enough for Steve to bear at one time. The sneer was too much. When he saw it, something snapped in his mind. He looked at Bubsy wide-eyed for just a split second, then his nostrils flared, his eyes glazed over, his face twitched convulsively and all the muscles in his body contracted at the same time. For an instant, it looked for all the world as if he were about to change into a very nasty kind of werewolf.

Bubsy took one look at him and realized that he'd pushed his brother too far. He closed his eyes at the terrible sight and took a small step backwards.

"All right wimp, you asked for it!" Steve screamed. "Now watch this!"

With the palm of one hand, presented in straight-arm fashion, he sent Bubsy staggering across the room and onto his rear end. Then he reached for the chair and threw it to the middle of the room. He jerked it upright, leaped onto it and reached for the ceiling.

"What are you doing!" Bubsy cried.

"What does it look like?" Steve said with hot white fury. "I'm taking them down. And if you say one word about it, I'll break your scrawny neck!"

But Bubsy was not afraid of his threats.

"You can't take them down!" he screamed. "MOM! DAD! He's trying to take my posters down!!"

At that moment Steve leaned back to remove a tack in the far corner of the Saint Bernard poster. In fact, he was leaning back a little too far. Bubsy saw the chair start to tip.

"Look out!" he cried.

His shout so startled Steve that he momentarily lost the little that remained of his balance and he started to fall. One leg went high in the air as he and the chair tipped over together.

"Help!" he cried.

Bubsy watched in horror as his brother came thundering down backwards onto the card table —and onto the model.

The huge balsa wood model airplane was instantly flattened. But worse was yet to come. The card table was never meant to take the weight of a human body falling on it from a height. And so, under the sudden impact of Steve's body, all four of its skinny legs began to collapse sideways...

Steve and the card table came down together in a steep, arcing motion, at the end of which Steve was slammed against the bookcase. The whole house shuddered from the impact. Meanwhile, up on top of the bookcase, the giant globe of the world wobbled round and round...

For the next fraction of a second, Steve just sat there, blinking and staring blankly into space. Meanwhile, on top of the bookcase, the huge globe wobbled right up to the edge of the shelf. It completed one more wobble, then it toppled off...

"Look out!" Bubsy cried.

Too late. At the same instant that Bubsy shouted his warning, the huge globe landed dead-centre on Steve's head. Such was its weight and such was the force with which it hit his skull, that the globe should have shattered into a thousand pieces. However, this was not the kind of globe that shatters very easily. It was made of very heavy metal. And so it merely bounced off Steve's head with a sickening, metallic clunk. Then it rolled over to Bubsy's feet, where it finally came to rest with Africa facing upwards. There was a serious dent in the middle of Africa.

"Steve?"

Bubsy feared the worst. But by some miracle, Steve did not appear to be dead. There were still minor signs of life. His eyes were blinking as he lay amongst the debris.

The giant model airplane was not so fortunate. It was definitely dead. When everything came to rest, a million tiny pieces of balsa wood covered Steve from head to toe.

His brother was still in a state of shock when their mother and father arrived. They stared in horror at him lying there in the wreckage. He was saying the same words over and over…

"My model. My model. My model…"

"Can I get a new card table to do my home-work on?" Bubsy asked them.

They didn't reply. They just stared at him. Then they stared at each other.

As it turned out, Steve was not badly hurt by the accident. However, he did have a rather bad headache and he did crack a small bone in his foot—in the other foot, as it turned out. When he came back from the clinic the next morning, there was a look of defeat and woe on his face. There was also a huge new cast on his foot.

"Can I sign your cast this time?" Bubsy asked him.

"Keep away from me!" Steve shouted. There was a glint of fear in his eyes.

Bubsy wandered outside, where he found his father driving wooden stakes into the ground directly behind the house.

"What are these for?" he asked, looking around at the stakes.

"They mark where the foundation will be," his father grunted as he hammered the last stake into the ground.

"What foundation?" Bubsy asked.

"For the new addition," his father replied.

"New addition?"

"Yes. Your mother and I are going to build a bedroom for a crazy little character who lives in our house."

"You mean… Is it going to be for me?" Bubsy asked, his eyes wide with sudden hope.

"Who else?" Mr. McGourlic said gruffly. While Bubsy stared at him with a stunned expression, a big grin spread over his father's face.

"Oh Dad!!" Bubsy cried. He rushed to his father and flung his arms around his neck.

When his mother came out a second later, she held out her arms to him. He threw himself at her and hugged her and kissed her.

"Oh, thanks Mom! Thanks! Thanks!" he cried out joyously.

"Go thank your aunt Kate," she suggested with a wry smile.

Before he could leave to do just that, his father placed his big hand on Bubsy's shoulder and looked gravely down at him.

"Do you know why we gave in?" he asked.

"Because you love me," Bubsy responded.

"No," his father said with a smile. "It's because we'd like Steve to live long enough to graduate from Junior High."

The End